For The Love of Old Bones

D0369556

Michael Jecks

Table of Contents

THE CORONER'S TALE

I'll always remember Sir Baldwin de Furnshill as he was in that dingy alley near the inn in Crediton. He was in his element, studying that corpse. Mind you, I prefer not to recall the scene in too much detail. I can still smell the sharp, rank tang of urine, the sweetness of putrefying fruit, the soft mustiness of the decaying dog's corpse. Next to them, the faint whiff of perfume from the slight body was like a breath of fresh air.

She was young – not yet out of her teens – and living I would have found her greatly attractive. Her body was still coltish, but her well-rounded figure was that of a mature woman, while her face had the same high brow and delicately arched eyebrows as my own good wife, partly covered by the long tresses of yellow-blond hair which had jerked from under her wimple in her final throes.

I shook my head. It wasn't difficult to infer what had happened. Like so many girls before her, and no doubt countless others who would follow, she had, probably unknowingly, fired a man's lust. 'It's easy to see how it occurred, Sir Baldwin,' I said. 'She was accosted here in the alley, and when she refused him, he tried to force himself on her. She tried to escape; he killed her.'

Sir Baldwin nodded, but I could see I wasn't holding his interest. His lean face with its neatly trimmed beard was focussed on the body. 'Murder, certainly,' he said heavily as he squatted, thoughtfully studying her hands. 'No rings, although this, her wedding finger, shows an indentation as if she wore one very recently. No purse either; both must have been stolen. She hasn't cut her hands, so she put up no fight. Perhaps he came upon her from behind and she didn't realise he was there.' He glanced up at me. 'Do you object to …?'

'Carry on,' I said, waving a hand dismissively.

Under my gaze he and his servant removed her tunic, wimple, undershirt and skirts, and left the girl naked under the sky. Slim and pale as marble where the moonlight caught her, she appeared almost to shine. For me, Sir Eustace of Hatherleigh, Coroner to King Edward II, in this, the fourteenth glorious year of his reign, the sight was nothing new, and yet it made me shake my head with sadness to see such beauty destroyed, ready only to be set kneeling in her grave, bowing to her God as she awaited the resurrection. I loathe to see waste of human life, but this in particular was painful. I couldn't help thinking of my own sweet Lucy, lying quietly at home in her bed at this moment, her little face so serene and peaceful in sleep. Lucy is twelve, almost old enough for her own husband, and surely only six or seven years younger than this child.

As I sighed and considered the pity of the life ended for so little reason, the knight rolled the small form over and over and exposed her back. He pointed to the stab wound, and I nodded again while the priest at my side crossed himself.

'Stabbed after being raped – or perhaps before,' the knight concluded as he stood, wiping his hands free of her blood on a piece of her clothing. 'And with a blade one inch wide at the thickest. It really is most difficult to find a murderer when we don't even know his victim's name,' he continued, frowning.

I nodded, but not without a slight sense of disappointment. It sounded as if he was not going to trouble himself over the case, and yet why should he? He'd been dragged here with me away from the great church hall where we had been feasting with the Dean to celebrate St Boniface's day. I was uncomfortably aware that the best of the food would already have gone while we stood there studying her small form. And even so he had managed to learn a little from her.

'She was no servant or villein. Her hands are unmarked, and if she had been used to menial work they would have been calloused.'

'I, Sir Eustace of Hatherleigh, Coroner, declare that this young woman was stabbed to death here on this evening, June the fifth, in the fourteenth year of our King, Edward the Second,' I intoned solemnly. I always find that making the formal statement helps the locals to come to terms with the discovery of a body, not that it mattered in this case. No one could possibly know her.

The people in this area were thin, hungry-looking tatterdemalions. This part of the town was inhabited by the poor, who eked out a living by helping farmers during the summer months and fighting for any humble work for the rest of the year. Their money would go on ale, while they would beat their children if they complained for lack of food. For the most part they were of the lowest class imaginable. If they'd possessed any pride or common dignity they would have gone to a manor and served a lord rather than live in such squalor. Surely the status of a villein would suit them better than filthy poverty. Yet some folk will always assume that freedom is better than serving a lord. They forget that freedom to live is often the same as freedom to die.

I think Sir Baldwin saw my look, for he gave a wry little smile. It made his face move oddly, twisting the side where a long scar ploughed the line of an old wound, running from temple to jaw. I've heard it said it was won in Acre many years ago when he fought to save that last Christian city in the Holy Land from the Moorish hordes, but I never dared ask him. Sir Baldwin gave the impression that he had an aversion to revealing his past, and such an enquiry would have been impertinent.

In any case, for all his vaunted understanding of human nature, he completely misunderstood my feelings about the citizens haunting the alley. They were all of them hanging around to see the body. It was right that the jury of fourteen should witness the body's inspection, but it was obvious that most of the men there that night were only satisfying a prurient interest; they inspired my contempt.

He waved a languid hand towards them. 'This child does not look as if she came from the same stock as these poor fellows, does she? They are all emaciated and worn down from their work, but look at her: well-fed and an easy life, if I am any judge,' he said softly in his quiet, contemplative voice. Then, casting an eye over the audience, 'Ralph, have you seen her before?'

The man to whom he called was one of a small crowd of townspeople. I had them waiting so I could get their names, for these men lived nearest the alley. That was the nice thing about my business in towns: it was always easy to find out who lived closest so that the fines for breaking the King's Peace could be imposed. Out of town things were often more difficult, especially when the locals refused to pay my fees, the ignorant cretins. One vill towards Tedburn refused to pay my charge, so I refused to view the body. By the time they agreed, the corpse was rotted, and to protect it they'd had to go to the bother of setting a hedge about it. I fined the lot of them double for wasting my time. You can't let these people get away with such wilfulness.

Looking at these folks again, I must say I wasn't impressed. Ralph was a sallow, gaunt-looking man in his early twenties, with fair hair that seemed to have dirt ingrained in it. The other neighbours were no better looking, all being wan, stooped, bandy-legged fellows.

Nearby was another huddle of locals, some of whom I recognised, like the tall and melancholy John, who owned a small alehouse on the Exeter Road. At his side was the innkeeper, Paul, greying and harassed, avoiding my gaze, nervously lifting his hand as if trying to conceal himself behind it. Standing behind them I could see the tranter, Edward. Usually a cheerful, confident little man, he kept his eyes fixed firmly on the body, his lips pursed in a thin line of anger. These churls are all the same; no doubt they all had their minds fixed on the fine they must pay.

Ralph shuffled forward, his head down. He mumbled for a moment, and I snapped at him to speak up. The trouble one has with these people!

'Sir Baldwin, I saw her here this afternoon going past my place, but never before that, I swear.'

'You were the first finder of the body, weren't you?' I demanded. It helps to keep a stern tone with his sort. 'You'll have to be amerced to make sure you come to the court. Give your details to my secretary here.'

He shuffled a bit more at that. I could see Sir Baldwin wanted to question him further, but to tell the truth I was more interested in getting back to the Dean's feast than staying out there in that dank and noisome alleyway. While Ralph muttered to the priest at my side, the townspeople gradually drifted away until we were almost alone. The innkeeper and his friends were all gone before Ralph had finished. Once he had, the knight spoke again.

'Ralph, tell me, which direction was she going in?'

'First time I saw her, she was walking towards Paul's place, the inn. She looked exhausted, like she'd only just arrived; her clothes were covered in the red dust you get on the roads around here, and she was stumbling a bit, as if she'd covered a lot of miles since daybreak. Later I saw her leaving Paul's and go down to the alehouse at the bottom of the hill. I reckoned she was looking for a place to stay the night.' He looked down at her sadly. 'Poor lass! She must have come here for the market, and this was her reward.'

'When was this, when you saw her?'

'A little before dark, because I had to go out to get rid of some rubbish, and it was while I was there by the gutter that I saw her the second time.'

'Was she alone?'

'Yes, sir. Paul came out and watched her, but so did I: she was such a pretty young thing, and yet seemed so sad. I watched her until she entered the alehouse.'

'That was the last time you saw her until you found her here?'

Ralph scuffed his shoes in the dirt, and Baldwin had to repeat his question before the man would answer, giving me an odd little sidelong glance. 'No, sir. I saw her again a while later, walking quickly up the hill to this alley. I was clearing up, and when I realised she hadn't come back again, I just thought I should make sure she was all right.'

'Did you see anyone else going in there?'

He shook his head, avoiding our gazes. 'Sorry, but no. No one else that I saw.'

'When she came into town, did she carry anything? A basket? Did she have a bag of goods to sell?'

'Nothing much, Sir Baldwin, only a small pack like a traveller would carry.'

'Then why did you think she was here for the market? Surely she would have brought something to sell? Even if she came here to buy, she would have brought something to carry off her purchases: a basket or a sack at the least.'

'Why else would she be here?' I interrupted reasonably.

'Perhaps when we know that, we'll know why she died.'

'Oh, Sir Baldwin!' I protested. 'She was obviously murdered by some drunk who met her in the alley, or maybe in the street itself, and who dragged her in here to molest her.'

'It is rare for a man to hurt, far less kill, a woman he has never met before,' said Baldwin confidently. 'I would think it far more likely that she was followed here to Crediton by a man she was trying to evade. He stabbed her in the alley because she wouldn't do what he wanted. Or perhaps that is the wrong way around, and in reality she was herself searching for a man, and when she found him, he struck her down.'

'I'm afraid I deal in facts, Sir Baldwin,' I said, a trifle brusquely I fear. 'If you want to invent a story, that's fine, but in the meantime I have to find out what I can for the inquest.'

'Shall we go and question the other men now, then?' he asked, and I thought I saw a gleam of amusement in his eye.

'We should wait until the morning for that,' I snapped. If we didn't get back there wouldn't be anything left to eat or drink.

The next morning I awoke with a head like a lead ball and a belly that roiled and bubbled as strongly as a witch's cauldron on all-hallow's eve. There was a constant taste of bile in my throat until I slaked my thirst with a pint of good strong wine and ducked my head into the water trough at the back of the Dean's stable. Then, dried and cleaned, I went to the hall to break my fast. There was cold meat in profusion, and I ate my fill of bread with thick slices of pork before heeding the request of the knight's servant that I should meet him near the alley. I confess I didn't see the need to hurry, and I drank off another pint of wine before making my way to see Sir Baldwin.

It was interesting for me to see how the knight worked. Of course, he didn't have the same position as me, for he was only a Keeper of the King's Peace, not a Coroner with all the powers that the title confers, but still his reputation was quite daunting. It was always said that criminals avoided his eye because he was so keen-witted and shrewd that he could see through a moorstone wall to a man's guilt, but rumours like that abound in a desolate little backwater like Crediton, so far from the bright life of court, so remote from civilisation.

'A good morning to you, Sir Baldwin. I hope I find you well?'

He uttered the usual courtesies, but I could see that his mind was concentrated on the dead girl. Soon we were discussing her.

'I can only assume she was looking for a means of earning money, if you are right and she didn't come here to buy or sell.'

He shot me a glance at that. 'You mean she was prepared to sell her body?'

'She may well have hoped that she wouldn't have to,' I said. I always like to give a young girl the benefit of the doubt, and it was only fair. 'But on arriving in the town and seeing how busy and bustling it was, no doubt the poor chit realised that any jobs would be filled by those who have always lived here. Who else would wish to employ a stranger? And after that realisation, what else could she do, I ask you? She needed money for food, for board, and to travel on to somewhere else. Maybe to Exeter? What else could she do but try to sell her body? And I fear that her first client saw her and stabbed her.'

We were almost at the door of the alehouse as I spoke, and I looked up at the small uprooted bush that dangled over the door. 'You want to go in here?'

He grinned at my distaste. 'I have drunk good ale in here many times before, Coroner. We have to try to discover what happened to the girl when she came in here.' And so saying, he ducked his head beneath the lintel and entered.

I need hardly say that I was not used to frequenting such low, mean dwellings, and would have protested at the thought of going inside, but with Sir Baldwin's servant standing behind me, I felt I had little choice. The man was oddly threatening. With a sense of chagrin, I followed Sir Baldwin.

Inside there was already quite a collection of rough, brutish men sitting on benches and supping their first whet of the day. All stared as I stood there, my eyes becoming accustomed to the dim light, which wasn't easy. The room had a small fire, but this early the air was still so chill that the smoke hung heavily above the hearth, and there was only one window in the opposite wall to permit a tiny shaft of sunlight. I heard a scrape of metal, as of a knife easing in its scabbard, but before I could move my hand to my own dagger's hilt, Sir Baldwin's servant moved past me, his own blade spinning in the air. He caught it and held it by the tip, ready to throw. When I glanced at his face there was an utter deadness to his eyes. They were as cold and unfeeling as a lizard's. A snake's. The room was quiet for an instant, and then the men at their tables began to murmur quietly to each other, studiously ignoring we three strangers.

Sir Baldwin appeared entirely oblivious to the brief tension. He was leaning at the doorway in the farther wall, talking to a tall, grave and lugubrious man.

'Sir Eustace, this is John, who owns this establishment.'

The innkeeper barely acknowledged me, beyond a short nod. His attention was fixed on the knight, with, or so I felt, a degree of nervousness as well as respect. 'She did come in here, sir, yes, quite early in the evening. A right pretty little wench she was, too, not much older than my own. Came here asking for a room. Said she'd already been to the inn, but that they charged too much for a room. I said to her, "This is no place for a gentlewoman," but she insisted. Had tears in her eyes, she did. Almost thought she'd go down on her knees to me. Said she couldn't afford another place to stay, and begged me to let her have a room.'

'You'll pardon my agreeing that your house is hardly the sort I would a girl to beg to stay in,' Baldwin noted.

The dour face cracked a grin. 'Sir, it's not the sort of place I'd expect a girl to look into, let alone walk in!'

'How can you be sure she was a gentlewoman and not merely some hussy?' I asked, and I must admit that I scoffed. His conviction about her status was ludicrous. As far as he was concerned she might have been a whore touting for trade in a new tavern.

He kept his eyes on Sir Baldwin as though I hadn't even spoken, the bastard. 'Her dress was worn and showed some hard use, but I think the dirt was recent. It was good cloth, and her face and hands were clean. Dust from the road had marked her apron and wimple, but her figure was good and full, not skinny from poor food, and her voice was confident enough. Yes, I'm sure she was well-born. As for her being a slut, well . . . I saw the way she walked in here, like it took all her remaining courage just to enter. She daren't even shoot the merest look at the men in here, for fear of bursting into tears, just strode up to me and kept her eyes on me, the poor thing. There was nothing brazen about it.'

'Did she wear a purse?'

'No, not that I saw, Sir Baldwin. That was why she came here, I think, because she had no money on her to take a room in a better house. I took pity on her and said she could use one, and a meal, for the sake of St Boniface.'

'Did she take a room?'

'Yes. The small one behind the hall. It's near my own chamber, and I thought I could protect her if anyone got amorous overnight. But she left before anything happened.'

'When was this?'

'Just as night fell. Before the church bell for the last service.'

Sir Baldwin nodded and thanked him, then stood abruptly and walked out. I found him with his hands hooked in his belt, leaning against a hitching post and glowering at the view.

'I know how you feel, Sir Baldwin. It's awful if she truly was a respectable woman, having to beg for a room in a place like this.'

'Hmm?' He gazed at me for a moment as if he didn't recognise me at all. Then a slow smile began to spread over his features. 'Oh, I see. No, I was just thinking that she must have come from that direction, from the east; if Ralph was right and she came past him, she must have been coming from that way.'

'So what? Does it really matter?'

'Perhaps not, Sir Eustace. But it means that she was walking in the wrong direction for Exeter. If she was some girl who had been running away from home, or, to take your example, if she was a whore looking for a new patch to work, she'd surely have been going the other way. No, she came here for a specific reason.'

'We're unlikely to discover what it might have been, though.' To be honest, I was finding his continual inferencing to be more than a little irritating. I was a Coroner, and had better things to do than stand in the street getting hot and dust-blown by passing traffic while my companion guessed at a range of different motives and explanations for how someone he had never known might behave.

'There is one thing that surprises me,' he muttered, this time peering over his shoulder westwards, towards the inn. 'Why should she come to town without money? Is it possible she was robbed on her way here? Or did she have some other reason to come here instead of staying in a decent, clean inn?'

'Who knows?'

'Let's go to the inn and ask Paul.'

If possible the innkeeper looked even more fretful and anxious than he had the night before. He had few enough customers this early, only a small number of tranters and hawkers and a couple of my own men, but insisted on calling his servants and ordering them about for some time as if demonstrating that he had much to do and couldn't spare a few minutes in idle chatter. Of course, that is often the way of men who are confronted by their Coroner. Our post is so important that it can cause the foolish to lose their tongues, so I didn't look upon his behaviour as suspicious. I merely waited, casting an interested eye over the women he had in there.

One was a real beauty: fair-headed, well-built under her tunic, from the look of her swelling chest, with a bawdy, excitable look in her bright green eyes. I made a mental note to return to see her when this silly affair was over.

When I cast a sidelong glance at Sir Baldwin, I was surprised to see him lounging and staring up at the ceiling. If I had to guess, I'd say he hadn't noticed the aproned idiot's play-acting. Sir Baldwin sat patiently until the innkeeper was ready, and then the stupid serf stood in front of us, asking in his whining, troubled voice whether we wanted a drink.

By this time I was hungry, and demanded a fresh meat pie. Baldwin seemed astonished by my desire for food, but he shrugged, merely asking for a quart of weak ale. The innkeeper scuttled away happily. It was so like a man of his class to hurry off when given an order by men of a higher standing. They need instruction, folk of his type, or they feel at a loss.

When he was back, and had hesitantly obeyed Sir Baldwin's next command and seated himself, the knight began his interrogation.

'The girl in the alley. I understand she was here yesterday afternoon?'

Paul licked his lips and glanced at both of us before studying his hands, clasped in his lap. 'Yes, sir, but only for a short time.'

'What did she do?'

'She came in late in the afternoon and asked for a room, Sir Baldwin. I saw her myself, and I was sure that she was a real gentlewoman.'

'You were? Yet she came here alone, without a horse or companion. What made you think she was ought but a common vagrant?'

'Oh, she had a real presence about her, Sir Baldwin,' he said, looking up at last. 'And her purse was filled with good money. I asked her whether she had coin on her, and she showed me – it was full.'

'When we found her body, there was no purse,' Baldwin commented.

The publican glanced at me and nodded. 'It must have been stolen,' he said miserably.

I stirred. 'All too often these people will steal after they have killed, you know, Sir Baldwin. You and I don't suffer from want, but common villeins in a neighbourhood like this would slit the throats of their own mothers to win an extra penny.'

He ignored me, which I have to say was damned insulting. His attention was fixed on the man before him. 'She showed you her purse; then what?'

Paul's gaze returned to his hands. 'Sirs, she came in exhausted, demanding a pint of watered wine, pleading a parched throat. I wanted to see her money before I went to fetch it, but when I saw how much she had, I brought her a jug . . .'

'And how did she appear? Happy, sad, anxious . . . ?'

'Oh, tired from her journey, but happy enough, I think. Later she got a bit nervy-looking. It was when Edward the Tranter came over and spoke to her. She got all flushed, like she was worried about something.'

'When was this?'

'Late afternoon, I suppose.'

'Did you overhear what Edward said to her?'

'No, sir. He spoke too quietly, and just after that she dropped some coin on the table and left with him, leaving her small pack on her stool. Later she came back for it, but by then she had this sort of lost look to her. I felt so sorry for her, I offered her a bed over the stables, but she just shook her head – didn't say a word, just shook her head, staring at me with her eyes all scared and sad, and her mouth a-quiver, like she was going to burst out in tears.' The innkeeper shook his own head as if in sympathy, studying the rushes at his feet, then looked up at Sir Baldwin. 'She saw or heard something that devastated her, sir. She thought her life was ended.'

His story struck a cold chill in my bowels and I felt the anger colouring my face. 'Do you think this Edward tried to force himself on her?' I demanded. 'If he did, by Christ's blood, he'll answer to me!'

'Oh, no, sir. I'm sure he'd not have done that. Edward's been coming here for donkey's years.'

'Was he drunk?' Baldwin asked quietly. I couldn't help but feel he thought my outburst was excessive, but then I must admit I was finding his coolness annoying.

The innkeeper gave a faint grin. 'You know Ed, Sir Baldwin! It'd be a rare day he wasn't a bit drunk. Still, he wasn't bitter or angry, just a little, well, thoughtful, I suppose.'

'Did you see where they went?'

'Yes, sir. I thought . . . Well, she was an attractive girl, and I couldn't help watching her. They went down the street a short way and into the alley near Ralph's place. The one where she was found last night. They went inside, but then I had to go to serve a customer. A while later she was back, took up her pack and went off. Ed came in a few minutes after her, and he went to his seat at the back. He stayed there for a good bit, before taking a game of dice.'

'Who were the other players?' Baldwin asked.

'The Coroner's men-at-arms, Sir Baldwin. I'm sure they'll remember him, he played with them for a long time.'

'When did he leave?'

'Early evening. One of the girls spent her time trying to tempt him, but he told her to piss off, and walked out.'

'So by now he was more bitter? In his cups he became angry?'

'I suppose so, Sir Baldwin. But like I say, he left here long after her.'

Sir Baldwin led the way to the street. There he paused and motioned to his servant, spoke to him quietly, and sent him off on some errand. Sir Baldwin and I began to make our way back to the Dean's house, but to my surprise he turned off and instead headed back towards that damned alley. By now Sir Baldwin's attitude was making me quite warm. The man was deliberately taking over my inquest, and wouldn't even explain what he was up to. I tried to control my growing annoyance, but I think a little of my feeling must have come across from the way he stopped and stared at me.

'Is there something the matter, Sir Eustace?' he asked.

'Yes, there is,' I declared hotly. 'God's bones! What in the name of hell are you going down here for?'

He began to walk again. 'I have an inclination that we might see something in daylight which we missed before. Clearly the girl had her purse stolen or she mislaid it between leaving the inn and going to the alehouse. I merely wonder whether she might have lost it here.'

I kicked a pebble from my path, but there was little to say. His decision was logical, and the purse had to be somewhere. Like him, I knew that most thieves would drop a purse once they had emptied it. There was no point keeping hold of something which could prove guilt.

It was only a short way from the inn, and soon we were in the gloomy corridor. The place where her body had lain was scuffed and muddy from all the feet which had come to see where she had died, and I was confident the knight was wasting his time. I leaned against the wall while he probed and searched. Then he gave a short exclamation, and sprang towards me, snatching something from the ground at my feet.

'What is it?' I asked, and in answer the grinning knight held out a small circle of yellow metal, crusted with mud.

'So the thief dropped her ring as he fled?' I suggested. His look sent a shiver of expectation trickling down my spine.

He ignored my words and peered at the wall. It was of cob and had probably been the outer wall of a house, but now it simply enclosed a garden. Baldwin turned and returned to the street, going to the front door and asking the bemused owner if he could go into the garden. As we walked through the little house, he gave me a dry little smile. 'If someone stole her purse, he may well have taken out all the coins and thrown it, empty, over the nearest wall. That would be sensible, wouldn't it?'

I grunted. As far as I was concerned the man was a fool, wasting my time as well as his own. I saw no reason to alter my opinion when we arrived in the yard. Sir Baldwin crouched and scrabble amongst the weeds near the wall. And then, to my astonishment, he lifted up her purse. I couldn't mistake it.

He hefted it in his hand, head on one side as he surveyed me. 'It's still full, Coroner,' he said softly, and there was a chill coldness in his voice and manner which I didn't like. But I felt it would be better not to take umbrage. Saying no more, he turned away and stalked from the place.

We had only gone a short way down the street when it happened. I should have expected it, of course, but when the tranter shouted and pointed at me, it was still a shock.

'Murderer! Bigamist!'

The blood turned to ice in my veins, my bowels felt as though they had turned to water, and I swallowed and retreated before the accusing finger Edward pointed at me. He had been waiting with Sir Baldwin's sergeant; obviously the knight had sent his man to fetch the tranter so that he could accuse me in this way. In the middle of the street, mark you!

'What do you mean by pointing at me? Do you dare to suggest . . .?' I blustered, but the man leaned forward and spat at me.

'Look at him, Sir Baldwin, a noble knight he'd have you believe, but he's a murderer of women! He has his wife at home, but he desired this young girl, so he swore his vows to her and enjoyed her nuptial bed, and then deserted her. And now he's murdered her to stop her spreading word of his faithlessness and deceit!'

The Dean was kind. He refused to allow the inquest to continue until I had drunk a full pint of wine, and I gratefully swallowed the jug in two draughts. I hadn't expected my secret to be so speedily discovered. When I had drunk, the Dean sat on a bench and Sir Baldwin motioned to his servant, who walked from the room - I thought to fetch more wine - before speaking.

'Now, Edward, perhaps you could tell us why you made your accusation?' Sir Baldwin was seated in the Dean's own chair across the table from me, the purse and ring before him, and I could almost feel his look, as if his eyes were shooting flames at me.

'I knew the girl. Her name was Emily, daughter of Reginald, a merchant in Tiverton. I used to have dealings with her father, and met her at the inn yesterday afternoon. She was tired, but thrilled to be here in Crediton, and I asked her if her father was with her. She went quiet at that, and said he wasn't. I pressed her, but she wouldn't say much, only soon she admitted she'd married a man by exchanging vows, but her father wanted her to wed someone of his choosing, and she left home rather than tell him what she'd done.'

The Dean nodded. 'If the two exchanged vows, the marriage was legal and valid, even if they did not have the banns read or have a priest witness their nuptials.'

'Yes, it was valid, sir, except she confessed that her lover was the Coroner, and this Coroner of ours is married, with a daughter. I realised immediately what had happened. Emily was a beautiful girl, Sir Baldwin. Any man would be proud to possess her, and this one wanted her all the more because she wouldn't satisfy his lust without a legal marriage. So he swore to her, and took her, and left her. And yesterday I had to tell poor Emily that he was married. She was desolate. Can you imagine it? Her lover had lied; she had lost her maidenhead to a man who could never be hers. For him she had forsaken her father and her family.'

'What do you say to this, Coroner?' Sir Baldwin demanded.

'It's rubbish! How can you trust to the word of a man like this? I . . .'

The blasted tranter cut me short. 'Sir, another thing is, this Coroner met her while he was in Tiverton performing the inquest on a girl who'd been stabbed in the market.'

'You cannot suggest that I had anything to do with that,' I cried. 'Christ's pain! It was two days after the murder that I arrived in town!'

'You were there all the time,' he countered, 'staying with the de Courtenay family at the castle.'

It was true, and there was no way I could deny it with conviction, but I still appealed to Sir Baldwin. 'Sir, you must believe me when I say that I had nothing to do with this murder! I couldn't have killed the poor girl. I loved her!'

That brought a chilly comment from the Dean. 'And what of your wife, Coroner? What of her whom you should have loved before you ever perjured yourself to this poor child?'

'Dean, I loved her! My wife and I have been married for years . . . You can't understand, your vow of chastity has emasculated you, but a man like me can love many women and . . .'

'Enough!' Sir Baldwin snapped. 'There is no need for you to say more, it is clear that you accept your bigamy.' He turned to Edward again. 'You have done well to bring all this to my attention, yet I would like to hear why you are so convinced that he killed her as well.'

The tranter took a deep break. 'After I spoke to her, she was devastated. She said she would speak to the Coroner. I said to her it would be foolish, but she begged me to intervene on her behalf, to speak to one of the Coroner's men at the inn and demand a meeting between them. When she went to fetch her stuff from the inn, I sat back and thought about it long and hard, but finally did as she asked. Back at the inn I got into a game of dice with some of the Coroner's men, and explained what had happened. The fellow gave me to believe it wasn't the first time something like this had happened, and agreed to ask the Coroner to meet her near the alley where she was found.'

'That's true enough,' I said, trying to demonstrate my innocence by assisting, but all I got was a chilly stare from Sir Baldwin, and I subsided.

'He promised that the Coroner would be there late in the afternoon, and I saw her as she left the inn and told her where to go. She thanked me, and went down to the alehouse, fearful of meeting someone she might know, if she stayed at the inn, and she concealed her purse when I suggested it. An alehouse is not the place to take lots of coin. She laughed then, sort of bitter. Said it wasn't hers now anyway. I . . . I also decided to go to the alley and see if she was all right. I was worried. I thought he might harm her.'

'What did you see?' Sir Baldwin asked quietly, his eyes on me.

'Sir, I found them right where her body was later. She accused him, and he confessed, sneering . . .' I felt the priest's cold, angry eyes fix upon me '. . . and said he would pay her to go away. Said she should go back to her father and not waste the King's Coroner's time. She dropped to her knees in the dirt and begged him to help her, but he laughed. Said he'd already paid her a small fortune, more than he'd paid a whore before! She said she'd thought the purse of money was so that she could go and set up home for them both, and he laughed again, saying it was just the price of her virginity. That was when she stood and started throwing things at him, calling him every name under the sun. He looked touched by her rage and misery, and apologised. I heard him promise her more money if she'd stop her crying. They were walking towards me now, so I ducked into a dark corner until they'd passed, then left. I needed a drink to wash away his deceit.'

I must confess to a vague sense of disinterest in the matter now. Maybe it was the wine, but it was as if all rationality had left me, and I was merely the shell of a man observing the destruction of another. I found myself biting my nails, bleakly watching the knight and priest with bland unawareness. It was as though all my reasoning abilities had flown.

Sir Baldwin nodded, drumming his fingers on the table before him. Shielding his eyes, he said, 'You went back to the inn, I suppose?'

'No, the alehouse owned by John and his wife.'

'And you did not see her again until you saw her body?'

'That's right.'

Now Sir Baldwin frowned at the table top before him. 'Is there anything you want to add, Sir Eustace?'

'It's a lie,' I spat. 'The man's jealous of me because she wanted me, and he's prepared to lie to have me hanged! He hates authority! Look at him, you can see it in his eyes, for Christ's sake! I met her, it's true, but she had her purse on her, and she held it to me and told me to take it back because she couldn't keep it, not now, and that was when I left her. Her tears were painful to witness, so I left her and came back here to the church for the feast. I wouldn't have killed her! Why should I? What would have been the bloody point?'

There was plenty more I could have said, damning him, the miserable tranter, even the Dean, but I held my tongue and dumbly shook my head. The truth is, I was too appalled by my position to be able to think clearly at all, and seeing the loathing in the Dean's eyes, where the night before they had been full of respect and friendship, left me feeling shrivelled and withdrawn.

Sir Baldwin sat silently and stared, yes, stared at me, for a good long while. All the time the room was quiet, as if everyone there was waiting for him to decide on my sentence. I wanted to scream out, 'It's not true, it's all a lie!' but I knew there was no point. Even the brilliant Sir Baldwin wouldn't be able to prove my innocence, and, to be fair, it looked as if he had already made his own mind about my guilt.

He finally pulled his eyes from me with an apparent effort of will, and drew them down to the table-top once more. He pulled the little purse towards him and untied the strings.

'I believe you are innocent, Coroner,' he said, and with those words I felt a charge like a blast of gunpowder thrill my whole body. I staggered like a man punched, and couldn't help but let out a gasp.

'No!' The tranter shook his head in disbelief and gazed wildly from the knight to me, his mouth working in rage. 'You can't let him go! I told you he was there, and I saw her with him. Who else could have killed her?'

'You,' said Sir Baldwin equably without looking up. He up-ended the purse and tipped out a stream of copper coins. 'And this money is why.'

Well, I confess I began to wonder about his reasoning then. He sat there, sadly studying the small pile of cash before him, like a seneschal who has just been told a serf cannot pay more towards his rent. When he spoke, his voice came from far away, as if he was relating a story long rehearsed.

'The Coroner had no reason to kill the girl. Why should he? She could have embarrassed him, but what of it? From all I have heard of Sir Eustace, he is quite used to conducting affairs of the heart, and I expect his wife knows all about them. One more could hardly cause him or her any concern. So I can see no logical reason why he should murder the girl. Yet if he had killed her, he is not the sort of man who would leave all this money with her. You, Edward, say that they walked away together, yet they didn't. She died there on the ground.'

'Because he killed her!'

Sir Baldwin held up a handful of coins. 'The Coroner would not have left this behind.'

'He must have thrown it over the wall!'

'No. She did that. Shortly after throwing the ring in his face, just after he left her, in a fit of rage and despair.'

The tranter stared while Sir Baldwin allowed the coins to dribble through his fingers. 'No, if the Coroner had killed her it could only have put him at risk. He was used to paying for his women, and he expected her to take the money and start a new life. But she threw the ring at him. She was honourable and wanted nothing of his, once she realised how he had dishonoured her. That was why she threw away the money. Every coin was a reminder of his faithlessness. But you didn't know it had gone, did you, Edward? You saw the Coroner leaving and hid until he had passed, but you had one thought on your mind: the money! You had seen how much she had at the inn, and you thought it would be easy to slip your blade between her shoulders and take the lot for yourself. Especially since you could incriminate the Coroner at the same time. And perhaps enjoy her body as well.'

'No! He killed her, just like Susan in Tiverton . . .'

'But as soon as the Coroner left her, she chucked the purse over the nearest wall. You were hiding and did not see that. You thought she still had the money on her. But when she was dead, you found nothing on her. Not even her ring.'

'I never looked for her . . .' He stopped himself suddenly while Sir Baldwin nodded slowly.

'And you were in Tiverton, too, when the other girl died, weren't you?' he said.

As he spoke, his servant returned. In his hand he held a loose bundle which he untied before his master. There inside was my spare knife, and the man pulled it free from its sheath and held it to Sir Baldwin. The knight took it and studied it closely, then set it aside and picked up a second.

'That's mine – what are you doing with it?'

The panic in the tranter's voice was a warm, soothing balm to me. I could have sagged with relief as I saw the knight frown and pick at the hilt. He wiped his thumbnail over the base of the blade and looked up coldly. 'Edward, I accuse you of murder. You will be taken from here to the gaol to await your trial when the justices are next here. And God help you!'

Later I went to the Dean's buttery and poured myself some of his best Bordeaux wine. It sank down wonderfully, and when I heard the knight's footsteps, I immediately rose and waved to him to offer him some so that he could drink to my wonderful success and freedom. I called out about the blond girl at the inn, and said I'd give him the first opportunity to assault her defences, all in good jest, you understand, although I admit I had been thinking about her myself, her with the wayward-looking eye.

And that's the other thing I remember about the man: his intolerable rudeness. He must have heard me, but while I stood there, holding the jug high, he walked straight past me without a word, hardly even glancing in my direction.

I mean to say, it's not as if I'd done anything wrong, the arrogant bastard!

FOR THE LOVE OF OLD BONES

The sudden violence was a shock: swift and devastating. They came at us from all sides, and what were we supposed to do? We couldn't run; we couldn't hide. There was nowhere to conceal ourselves on that desolate damned moor.

I was struck down early. When I came to, it was to find my head being cradled in the lap of a rough countryman, a shepherd from the rank smell of him, holding a leather bottle of sour-tasting water to my lips that I drank with gratitude. All about me, when I felt able to gaze around, were my companions: resting, holding broken heads, or wincing as their bruised limbs gave them pain. It was all I could do to pull away and kneel, fingering my rosary as I offered my thanks to God for delivering us from our attackers.

"The Abbot is dead!"

The cry broke in upon my devotions and I had to stifle my gasp of horror. I saw Brother Charles at the side of Abbot Bertrand's slumped figure and hurried over to them as fast as my wounded head would allow.

Abbot Bertrand de Surgères, my lord, lay dead; stabbed in his back.

It is always difficult to try to recall small details after a horrible event. I and my English brethren have suffered much in the years since the great famine of 1315 to 1316. As peasants lost their food, so there was less for us monks; the murrain of sheep and cattle that followed devastated our meagre flocks and herds, and now, late in the year of our Lord thirteen hundred and twenty-one, I had myself taken my fill of despair.

With the pain in my head from the crushing blow, I was in no state to assist my brothers in tidying the body of our Abbot. I sat resting while they unclothed him and redressed him in fresh linen and tunic; others walked a mile or more northward to a wood, from where they fetched sturdy boughs to fashion a stretcher. The horses had gone, of course. For my part, I could not help them. I knew only pain and sadness as I watched them work.

It was a cold, quiet place, this. The sun was watery this late in the year, and its radiance failed to warm. We were on the side of a hill, with a small stream gurgling at our feet. A few warped and twisted trees stood about, but all were distorted, grotesque imitations of the strong oaks and elms I knew. The grass itself looked scrubby and unwholesome, while the ground held a thick scattering of rocks and large stones, giving the scene a feeling of devastation, as if a battle had raged over it all. It felt to me like a place blasted with God's rage. As it should, I thought, with one of His Abbots lying murdered on the ground.

The shepherd disappeared soon after I awoke, but while my companions set the Abbot's body on the stretcher and began gathering together the few belongings that the robbers had scattered, I sat quietly. I saw Brother Humphrey pick up the Abbot's silver crucifix. He saw my quick look and smiled weakly. In our little convent there have been occasions when odd bits and pieces have gone missing, and he knows I suspect him. The cord of the cross was broken, although the cross and tiny figure were fine; nearby, Abbot Bertrand's purse lay on the ground. Humphrey picked up both and passed them to me with a puzzled expression.

As he stood there, I heard hoofs. Looking up, I saw three men at the brow of the hill. One was the shepherd, the other two were on horseback. They were unknown to me; indeed, I could hardly make out their features for the low, autumnal sun was behind them, and it was hard to see more than a vague shadow. Now, of course, I know Bailiff Puttock of Lydford and his friend Sir Baldwin of Furnshill near Cadbury, but then they were only strange, intimidating figures on their horses, staring down at us intently while the shepherd leaned on his staff.

At the sight of them Humphrey let out a cry of despair, fearing a fresh attack; a pair of servants grabbed their staffs and advanced, determined to protect us. The three remaining brothers began reciting the Paternoster; me, I simply fell to my knees and prayed.

The men rode down the incline and I could make them out. It was soon obvious that one of them was a knight - his sword belt and golden spurs gleamed as the sun caught them. His slow approach was reassuring, too. It gave me the impression that we were safe: he hardly looked like one of the predatory knights who might conceal robbery by making demands in courtly language. In any event, such a one would have brought a strong party of men-at-arms to steal what they wanted.

"Brothers, please don't fear us," the other man said as he neared the staffman. "I'm Bailiff Puttock under Abbot Champeaux of Tavistock Abbey and my friend is Sir Baldwin, the Keeper of the King's Peace in Crediton. This shepherd told us of the attack and we have already sent for the Coroner to view the body. May we help you?"

I heaved a sigh of relief. There was no fearing men such as these. "Godspeed, gentlemen! It is an enormous relief to meet you. Now at least we need fear no footpads while on the moors."

It was the knight who spoke first, studying me with an oddly intense expression, like one who has no liking for monks. He was tall, with heavy shoulders and a flat belly to prove that he practiced regularly with his sword. Intelligent dark eyes glittered in a square face with a thin beard that followed the line of his jaw. One scar marred his features, twisting his mouth. "Your name, Brother?"

"I am Brother Peter, from Launceston Abbey. My Abbot sent me to help our brethren on their arduous journey to France and back. We were on our way to Launceston when this happened."

"It's a long way to go without horses, Brother," the other man pointed out.

"We had horses until last night, when they were taken."

"You were robbed? God's teeth! The thieving bastards!" Bailiff Puttock burst out. "How many were there? And which way did they go?"

"I was knocked down early on," I grimaced, gingerly feeling the back of my tonsure. The skin was broken slightly and there was a large lump forming that persuaded me not to prod or probe too hard.

"There were six of them. They appeared like devils as the sun faded, running straight at us ..."

As I spoke I could recall the horror. Screaming, shrieking men, all wielding staves or clubs, springing down from the surrounding rocks, belabouring us, holding us off while two young lads, scarcely more than boys, took our horses. And a short while later, nothing: they had clubbed me.

The knight was silent, but the Bailiff cocked his head. "None of them had a knife?"

"I don't recall. My head - I was unconscious."

"What was their leader like?"

"Heavyset, bearded, with long dark hair."

"I have heard of him."

"They took most of our provisions as well as our mounts."

Sir Baldwin walked off a few yards, bending and studying the ground. He went to the stream and followed its bank a short distance, then round the curve of the hill, disappearing from sight.

His friend appeared confused. "You say these men attacked and took your horses - but only your Abbot was stabbed? It seems odd…"

He would likely have added more, but then his friend called, "They went this way. Their prints are all over the mud at the side of the stream. It looks like they have gone westward."

"Which is where we should go as well," Bailiff Puttock said. "If there are thieves on the moors we should warn the abbey. We can send a second messenger to the Coroner explaining where we have gone."

"And it would be a good place for these good brothers to recover from their ordeal," Sir Baldwin agreed.

"It seems curious that the thieves should have left such wealth behind."

We were resting in a hollow on the old track to Tavistock. All of us were tired after our ordeal and needed plenty of breaks. The knight was squatting, studying the crucifix and purse.

The Bailiff shrugged unconcernedly. "They grabbed what they could."

"But they killed an Abbot."

"So? In the dark they probably didn't realize he was an Abbot, nor that they had killed him. It was a short, sharp scuffle in the gloom."

"Hmm."

I could see that the knight wasn't convinced. The Bailiff, too, for all his vaunted confidence, scarcely seemed more certain. Both stared down at the items. I cleared my throat and held up the cold meat in my hand. "Could one of you lend me a knife? My own was still on the packhorse."

With a grunt the knight pulled a small blade from his boot and passed it to me.

"I've known thieves leave behind goods after being scared off," Bailiff Puttock continued after a while.

"And I have known Bailiffs who have left wine in the jug after a feast - but that does not mean I have ever seen you behaving abstemiously. No, these robbers planned their raid. Two things are curious: first, that they bothered to kill the man; second, that they left his wealth at his side."

"Who were these robbers, Sir Baldwin?" I interjected.

"We may never catch them, Brother," he said with a smile. "There are so many who have been displaced since the recent wars in Wales. They have swollen the ranks of the poor devils who lost everything during the famine."

"Poor devils, my arse!" Puttock growled. "They should have remained at their homes and helped rebuild their vills and towns, not become outlaw and run for the hills."

"Some had little choice," Sir Baldwin said.

"Some didn't, no, but this gang sounds like Hamo's lot again."

"They've never killed before," Sir Baldwin said slowly.

"True, but the leader sounds like Hamo and the theft of the horses is just like his mob."

Sir Baldwin rose. "This is not helping us. You saw nothing of five and the death of your Abbot, Brother Peter?" I shook my head. "Then France, let us ask your friends. Could you introduce us?"

I nodded. "Brother Humphrey is another Englishman like me, but Brother Charles comes from France. He is the shorter of the three. The third, the handsome young one, is Brother Roger, who is also French. He comes from the Abbot's own convent."

"What was the reason for their visit?" the Bailiff asked.

"There has been debate for many years about where certain relics should be stored. The fingerbone of Saint Peter is held at Launceston and I was sent to the Abbot to explain why we felt it should remain," I told him sadly.

My head throbbed again with the recollection of that dreadful meeting. It was held by Abbot Bertrand in his chapter house, and the place reeked. The fire's logs hadn't been properly dried and the hearth in the middle of the room smoked foully, filling the place with an acrid stench; censers competed with it, with the result that all of us were coughing by the end of the meeting - if it could be so termed. We discussed the ins and outs of sites for the bones, but the decision had already been made. That was made abundantly clear. Our carefully thought-out arguments were overruled or ignored.

"They could think of taking such a relic back to France?" Sir Baldwin asked with frank astonishment.

I allowed a little acid into my voice. "It's the way of the French. Now that they have installed the Pope in Avignon they feel that they can win any argument they wish."

"But to take the bones from a place like Launceston! It is not as if there is much else for the people to venerate there!"

"No, indeed. Launceston is far from civilization. It is an outpost on the fringes of society; without the few items we have, how can we hope for God's grace to protect us?"

Bailiff Puttock watched the men. "And you say that this Brother Charles is French? Let's ask him about last night."

My friend Brother Charles was a short, thickset man of maybe five-and-twenty years. Originally from the southern provinces of France, near the border with Toulouse, his tonsure was fringed with sandy coloured hair. Upon being called to meet with the knight and his comrade, Brother Charles appeared nervous, as if he feared their presence.

Bailiff Puttock spoke first. "I hear you're from a French Abbey, come here to remove English relics?"

Brother Charles threw me a helpless look. "I was commanded to join my Abbot, it is true.

"To take away bones from Launceston?°

"That was the plan. The mother-abbey has need of them."

"So does Launceston," the Bailiff snarled gruffly.

"My Abbot decided. I was ordered to join him together with my friend Brother Roger and these other good monks, Humphrey and Peter, from the monastery of Launceston."

"Very well. What happened last night?"

"My Lord, I was preparing some pottage for our evening meal when I heard a shout. It was one of the grooms. I looked up and saw him toppling over. A great bear of a man stood behind him, grasping a heavy staff. It was awful! I was about to rush to help the groom when I realized there were more attackers. I thought it better to go to the Abbot's side and help defend the camp."

"Where was everyone else?" Sir Baldwin asked.

"I can hardly recall, Sir Baldwin. It is all so confused in my mind. The men attacked so swiftly ... I was at the fire when I heard the first scream. When I turned I saw Brother Peter crumple. Abbot Bertrand still had Brother Humphrey and Brother Roger with him. There was so much shouting - so many cries and screams. One of our servants was felled and then I realized a man was near me, the same gross fellow who had hurt Brother Peter. I avoided his club and went to my Lord Abbot's side.

"But when I got there, two men rushed at us, and I only had time to grab a stick and thrust at them, but missed, I fear. I was knocked back, driven toward the fire again, fearing all the time that the big man who had knocked Brother Peter down could strike me from behind. The Abbot fell. I saw him, I think. It was all so confused! Then they were pulling away, and we heard the sound of our horses cantering away. The men laughed as they scurried off. And I saw my Abbot on the ground."

"Did he say anything?"

"No. He was dead. The blade that struck him down killed him instantly. He made no sound."

"How close was he to you?"

"He was only a few yards from me." Brother Charles belatedly realized that the questioning was focusing unpleasantly upon him. "But we had all gathered close to each other."

Sir Baldwin held up his hand. "Do not worry yourself. We only wish to see the place through your eyes. Tell me, what was the Abbot like?"

Brother Charles threw me a confused, desperate look, and I interjected, "Sir Baldwin, what has this to do with his death? Surely, it would be better for us to continue on our way and warn others of these thieves before they can harm other travellers?"

"Yes, but please humour us. This Abbot of yours - was he a generous, kindly fellow?"

I gave a brittle smile. One should hardly speak ill of the dead, but ... I chose the path of least trouble. "He was deeply religious and devoted to his abbey."

Sir Baldwin eyed me with a faint grin. "He was not your friend, then."

There was no need for me to say anything. I merely hung my head.

"Was it the bones?"

I met his eye with stern resolution. "Sir Baldwin, I feel that your questions are bordering upon the impertinent. You are questioning me

30

about a matter that is of little, if any, concern of yours. An Abbot has been murdered and that offense falls under Canon Law. It is not within your jurisdiction. However, we do have a responsibility to others to see to their protection. For that reason I should like to hurry to Tavistock. In addition, I have to take the good Abbot's body to the abbey for burial. Should we not continue on our way?"

The way was hard. Devonshire has few good roads. All of them involve climbing hills and dropping into rock-strewn valleys with few good bridges over the chilly, fast streams. It was a miracle that none of us broke an ankle on the treacherous soil or fell into one of the foul-smelling bogs.

The knight and his friend were good enough to lend their horses, one to me, one to poor Brother Roger. He, too, had been struck down in the attack, and he rode slumped, his head rocking as if he were dozing. Once I had to hurry to his side and hold him upright when he all but fell from the saddle.

After that I felt I had little option but to accede when the Bailiff suggested that we should stop again. It led to my feeling fretful and irritable, but I could see no alternative.

We had come to a pleasant space in which strange buildings of stone abounded. They might have been ancient huts for shepherds like the man who had helped us and who now traipsed along gloomily. He had been told that he should join us so that his evidence could also be given alongside our own.

Many men worked the moors, I reflected. Miners scrabbled for tin, copper, and arsenic on the wildlands; farmers raised their sheep and cattle; builders dug quarries. All lived out there, in the inhospitable waste.

Yet none could be seen from here. The moor stretched five leagues, maybe, north and south of this point, and was at least four leagues wide. That was why gangs of thieves and outlaws could easily lose themselves. Even now they could be up there watching us, laughing as they sat astride our own ponies.

The thought made me shiver with anger. Knaves like them deserved to die!

The Bailiff and the knight approached Humphrey almost as soon as we had stopped, and I pursed my lips with annoyance. It was obvious that they intended to question him as they had Brother Charles, and I wasn't going to have it. Instead, I called Brother Humphrey to me, asking him to join me in prayer.

He did so with alacrity, and I smiled, glad to have rescued him. I also caught sight of the speculative expression on the knight's face. It was suspicious, as if he thought I was behaving oddly, but I didn't care. I took Humphrey's hand and led him away, sitting with him on a stone and murmuring the prayers for the office of Sext. It was surely about noon.

While we prayed and offered ourselves once more to God, I saw Brother Roger walking away to fetch water. It was a relief, for I was sure that as soon as they could, the knight and the Bailiff would be after him as well with their questions.

Finishing our prayers, I patted Humphrey's arm and he gave me an anxious smile in return. Poor Humphrey was plainly scared. His pale grey eyes were fearful, darting hither and thither like those of a hunted animal. The affair was taking its toll on the nineteen-year-old, and I gave him a reassuring grin.

I was about to offer him some advice when he stopped me. "Last night - I have to tell someone ..."

"Shh!" I hissed. I could sense the two pests approaching. Their shadows loomed.

"Brother Humphrey, we'd like to ask you what you saw last night," Bailiff Puttock said.

The knight hunkered down beside us. "It's hard to understand why the Abbot should have died. Especially since he had money on him, money that was not taken but was instead left at his side. Did you see him stabbed?"

"No, Sir Baldwin. I could scarcely see anything."

"You weren't knocked unconscious?" the Bailiff asked.

"No."

"You came from Launceston with Brother Peter here, didn't you?"

"Yes. We were both sent to persuade the Abbot against taking our relics."

"But he decided to in any case?"

"They wouldn't listen to us!" Humphrey stormed. "It wasn't fair! They'd already decided to steal our ..."

I interrupted hastily. "This was no theft, Humphrey. It was their right and their decision."

"The relics are ours! They should remain in Cornwall!"

"Did you like the Abbot?" Sir Baldwin asked.

Humphrey looked at me, and I glanced at the knight with an annoyed coldness. "Sir Baldwin, what has this to do with anything? The Abbot - God bless his soul! - is dead. What good can raking over other people's feelings for him achieve?"

"Brother, you were unconscious and couldn't have seen much," Bailiff Puttock said easily, "but we have to find out as much about these robbers as we can because we have to catch them. All we want is to gain a good idea of exactly what happened last night."

Before Humphrey could answer, I peered over my shoulder. Brother Roger had not returned. "Go and seek Brother Roger. I fear he could have become lost. God forbid that he should be swallowed in a mire."

When he was gone, I faced the two once more. They exchanged a look.

"Brother Humphrey is well known to me, and I would prefer that you didn't question him too deeply. It could harm him."

"What's that supposed to mean?" the Bailiff demanded. "The man's fine, but you seem determined to protect him from our questions. Why?"

"Because he is not well," I told him harshly. "Good God! Can't you see? The fellow is a wreck."

"Because of the attack?"

I took a deep breath. "No, because his father was a clerk in Holy Orders who raped a nun. Humphrey is convinced that his whole existence is an affront to God."

"Christ's bones!" the Bailiff gasped. "The poor bastard!"

"So I would be most grateful if you could leave the poor fellow alone. He needs peace, and the attack itself has severely upset him. I should have thought that you would have been able to see that!"

The two apologized handsomely. It was plain that the Bailiff was shocked by what he had heard. And who wouldn't be? The story was one to chill the blood - being born as a result of the rape of one of Christ's own brides was hideous. It had marked out poor Humphrey from early on: the product of a heretical union.

"Did the Abbot know of his past?" Sir Baldwin asked.

"Yes. Naturally. Abbot Bertrand knew about all of us."

I saw the knight's attention move behind me and turned in rime to see Humphrey leading Brother Roger back into the makeshift camp. The Frenchman looked confused and happily took his seat on a satchel, while Humphrey solicitously spread a blanket over his knees and patted his hand. I called to him sharply and asked him to fetch a wineskin. We could all do with some refreshment.

Only a few moments after the knight and Bailiff had risen, they began to move in the direction of Brother Roger. I followed them, pointing out that the poor lad was dazed still from his wound.

"I understand that, but I would still like to ask him a little about the attack," the knight stated in what I can only call a curt manner. He was growing testy.

"There seems little need. I have told you what I saw, and you know who the killer is."

"You have told us that you did not see anyone stab him," the Bailiff said. "We still have to see whether anyone might have seen who actually did."

"Good God above! I told you about our attackers - what more do you want?"

"A witness who saw him shove a knife into your Abbot's back," he said shortly.

I could feel the anger twisting my features as I trailed after them toward the sitting monk, and I was forced to pray for patience in the face of what felt like overwhelming provocation.

Brother Roger was young, only perhaps twenty-two. Looking up with a mild squint against the brightness of the day, he had to keep closing his eyes as we spoke, as though the sun's light was too powerful for him.

"My friend, these men wish to ask you about the attack last night to find out whether you saw the leader of the outlaws stab ..."

The knight interrupted me. "Brother Roger, you were yourself knocked on the head. When did you waken?"

"This morning. I was unconscious for some hours. And my head!" He winced. "It was worse than the headache after an evening drinking strong wine!"

"What do you remember of the attack?"

34

I was near the Abbot, and when the first cry came to us, he was on his feet and rushing for the horses, but he was stopped. A group of the felons appeared, and we ran to the Abbot's side to protect him. I was there at his right hand," he added with a hint of self-consciousness.

"Did you see anyone stab him?"

"No."

Brother Charles had approached and now he interrupted. "I saw him crumple like an axed pig. One moment up and fighting; the next, collapsed in a heap. It was as if he had been struck by a rock."

"You are sure of this?" the knight pressed him.

"Oh, yes," Charles said emphatically. "He fell because he was struck on the head."

"One of the outlaws could have heaved a stone at him," the Bailiff said pensively.

"Perhaps," Sir Baldwin said. "Tell me, Brother Roger: the Abbot, was he always a bold man?"

"Very brave and courageous. He would always leap to the front of any battle. He had been a knight, you see. He was Sir Bertrand de Toulouse before he took Holy Orders."

Now Baldwin's brow eased. The frown that had wrinkled his forehead faded. "So that is why he was so keen to be at the forefront of the fighting!"

"Yes. He would always go to a fight to protect his own. And, of course, he saw a man attacking Humphrey," he added with a faintly sneering tone to his voice.

"Humphrey was sorely pressed?" Bailiff Puttock asked.

I shot the loathsome Frenchman a look of warning but he met it with sneering complacency. "No, Bailiff. Abbot Bertrand was a sodomite; he wished to preserve the life of the man he adored."

After he had let it out, there was little more for me to say. I walked away and left the knight and his friend still talking to the Frenchman, but I wished to hear no more of their inquiry. If they wanted more, they could come and find me.

I left the camp, seeking the stream that Roger had apparently discovered. It was a short distance away. Some twenty yards farther up was the corpse of a sheep, and as I drank I saw that it had horns still attached to its skull. As soon as I had drunk my fill, I walked up and pulled them off. They would decorate a walking stick.

It was relaxing here, listening to the chuckle and gurgle of the water. I rested upon a rock and stared at the water for a time, considering. So much had happened recently. There was the horror of finding that the Abbot wanted our relics, to help him persuade gullible peasants and townspeople to give him more money in exchange for prayers said within the church. The shock of learning that he had made up his mind before the arguments could be put before him. And last there was the terror in Humphrey's eyes when the Abbot had fondled and caressed him after the meeting, promising him wealth and advancement should he agree to share the Abbot's bed.

Humphrey had lost the veneer of calmness he had developed over such a long period. It had been appalling to him to discover that the Abbot was corrupt - perverted! How could he respond, he asked, and I told him: simply refuse and walk from the Abbot if he tried it again.

But now I had to cover my face in my hands at the result.

I arose preparing to return to the camp, when I heard the scream. Eerie, it seemed to shiver on the air as a gust wafted it toward me. It was as if a hand of ice had clutched at my heart. A trickle of freezing liquid washed down my spine, and I felt the hairs of my head stand erect.

All at once I remembered the stories of ghosts and demons on the moors. This grim wasteland was home to devils of all kinds who hunted fresh souls with their packs of baying wishhounds. This shriek sounded like that of a soul in torment, and my hand grabbed at my crucifix even as I mouthed the paternoster with a shocked dread.

Before I could finish, Sir Baldwin was at my side, his sword in his hand. "Where did it come from?" he rasped, staring northward from us.

For the second time that day, I was glad to see him, and for the second time I could tell him little. "Up there somewhere."

He gave me a twisted little grin. "This is hardly what a monk should be used to."

"I'm not!" I said grimly. The sight of his unsheathed sword had recovered a little of my courage. The blade was beautiful, fashioned from bright peacock-blue steel.

He motioned with it. "Shall we see what caused that noise?"

"Very well."

I had no desire to see this, but equally I had no wish to appear a coward. Also, if it were a human or mortal beast creating that unholy row, I would be safe enough with the knight; while if it were the noise of a devil seeking a soul, I should be as safe out in the moors as I was in the camp. Either way, I knew that however strong my faith should have been, I would feel happier with this armed man at my side.

"I've told the servants to guard the camp," Bailiff Puttock said, striding toward us. He carried a coil of rope over one shoulder.

"Good," Sir Baldwin said absently. "Brother Peter thinks the noise came from over there."

The Bailiff chuckled. "I'm afraid not. The wind can do odd things to sounds out here. No, it would have come from there." He pointed, and soon was leading the way.

The scream came again as we clambered over rocks and tussocks of loose grass. It was also damp. "What could that noise be?" I asked.

Bailiff Puttock cast me a smiling glance. "Haven't you got bogs near Launceston? It's the sound of a desperate man bellowing for help after falling in one of our mires. Not a nice way to die, that."

I realized then what my eyes and feet had been telling me. The ground here trembled underfoot as I placed my feet upon it, and the grasses each carried an odd, white pennant at the tip of their stems: this was no grass, it was a field of rushes.

"Watch my feet and step only in my own footprints," the Bailiff commanded.

I was happy to obey him. When I lost concentration for a moment, my leg slipped up to the shin in foul, evil-looking mud. I muttered a curse, and as I pulled my foot free, there came another cry. It scarcely sounded human.

We scrambled up to the top of a ridge, and upon the other side we had a clear view for some miles. There, at the edge of a field of white rush flowers, we saw a man's head. His arms were outspread and one gripped at something, a bush or twig.

"He's further gone than I'd thought," the Bailiff muttered before springing down the gentle incline, the knight, his sword now sheathed, and I stumbling along as best we could. At the base of the hill was a kind of path made of stepping-stones and we had to hop from one to another until we came close to the mire.

"Christ Jesus; praise the saints! Thank you, thank you, thank you!"

"My God!" I said. "It's him!"

The Bailiff grinned. "Meet Hamo!"

It took time to persuade the moor to give up its victim. When we finally hauled him from the filthy mud, he lay sprawled like a drowned cat rescued from a rain butt, as if he were already dead. Bailiff Puttock bound his arms with his rope. Soon Hamo gave a convulsive gasp, almost a sob, his face red and fierce after his struggle.

"The bastards," he wheezed. 'They threw me there to die, God rot their guts!"

"You," Sir Baldwin said mildly, "are arrested."

"What for?" the man demanded suspiciously.

"The murder of Abbot Bertrand," Bailiff Puttock said, firmly binding his hands. "You stole his horses last night and stabbed the Abbot when he lay on the ground."

Hamo shrugged expansively. "I'll hang for the horses, and you can only hang a man the once, but I never killed him. That was why my gang threw me in the mire to die, the bastards! Because they heard a rumour that an Abbot had been killed; but it wasn't me. I saw him fall like he'd been struck dead while we fought, but then there were two other men to worry about. I didn't have time to stab him. Do you know where the gang lives? I can take you there if you want to kill them." He shivered, casting a glance back at the mire.

"We'll think about it. Do you swear on your soul that you didn't kill the Abbot?" the Bailiff asked.

"I swear it on my soul and on my mother's soul. I never hurt the man. He fell before I could strike him."

It was clear that the two were impressed by his assertions. Sir Baldwin prodded him with his sword while the Bailiff gripped the rope's end, and I wandered along cautiously in their wake.

Returning we took a longer path, one which was, I am glad to say, less soggy than the one we had taken on the way to find this barbarous fellow. Before long we had got back to the camp and had bound our captive to a tree. He nodded and grinned to the men gathered there, but he was refused any wine or water from our stores. Since he had stolen our stocks, we reasoned it was hardly reasonable that he should take a share in what was left us.

"Why didn't you take the Abbot's crucifix?" the Bailiff asked.

"I didn't even see it. Look, there was a fight, right? I waded in quickly so that our boys could cur the horses free and lead them away. I stood against the Abbot, but he suddenly fell; when he did, I was beset by two more men. He grudgingly nodded toward Roger and Charles. "I didn't have time to feel the man's body. Almost as soon as he fell there was a shout and we withdrew. That's all I know."

"What of these others?" Sir Baldwin said, indicating Humphrey and me.

"I saw that one," he said, nodding toward me. "I hit him early on. Not hard, but he dropped. The other one - I don't remember."

"So you, Brother Humphrey, are the only one who not accounted for," Sir Baldwin said softly.

"Sir Baldwin, that is outrageous!" I roared. "Dare you suggest..."

"Quiet, father, let me ..."

The Bailiff's jaw dropped. "You...*you* are his father?"

I sank wearily to a rock and passed a hand over my forehead. "Yes," I admitted. "I was the evil fool who raped his mother, may God forgive me! And I murdered the Abbot."

"Father, no! It was me he insulted!"

"Bailiff, I know what I am saying," I said again. In truth, it was a relief to end the anticipation. "My son was in danger from the Abbot. I had to protect him. The Abbot wanted him to go to his bedchamber. He told me, and I sought to defend him as best I could." I stood and patted my son's shoulder. "When I saw the fight, it was as if I saw the means. I threw a stone at the Abbot hoping that he would falter and be struck down, killed. He fell, and I then went and stabbed him when no one else was watching."

"Interesting," Sir Baldwin said. "Yet you were yourself unconscious during the attack."

"I fell but I was only bewildered for a moment. As soon as I came to, I saw what was happening. There was a rock by my hand and I hurled it at him."

"And?" Bailiff Puttock asked.

"What do you mean, 'and'?"

"You threw the stone at him, jumped to your feet, and hurled yourself across the camp to stab him?"

"Yes," I said.

"Where is your knife?"

His words made me blink. I hadn't thought of that. I don't wear a knife. My eating knife was on the packhorse. I had already told them that. "My knife ... I dropped it after -"

"Father, stop it!"

I couldn't restrain him, my boy threw himself at my feet. "I didn't kill him and neither did you! You never threw a rock. You had collapsed! I saw you."

"So who *did* kill him?" I asked, and now, I confess, I was too astonished to be more than a little bemused by the course of events.

"*Him!*" Humphrey spat, pointing at Brother Roger. "When I saw you had fallen, I cried out. The Abbot thought I had been hurt and leapt to my side. Roger knocked the Abbot down in a fit of jealousy, and I think he stabbed the Abbot later when no one was watching."

"Me? Why should I do this?"

"Because the Abbot had thrown you over. He thought you pretty when you were a choirboy, and I suppose he loved you in a way, but then he wanted me instead, and you couldn't cope with that, could you?"

"I was fighting with *him*, and I fell, just as did your father."

"My father has blood on his head and a lump - what do you have?" Humphrey sneered.

It was with a sense of - I confess it - disbelief that I realized what my son had noticed. The Frenchman had said that he was dreadfully knocked, had taken a horse because of his supposed pain, and yet he had no bruise, no lump, no blood. And he could stand and debate with Humphrey.

As the thought came to me, I saw him stand, white-faced with rage. Suddenly, he whipped a hand beneath his robe and pulled out a knife. He launched himself on my boy.

I suppose I didn't think of the danger. All I knew was that my boy was at risk. Did I realize I was risking my own life? I don't know. Perhaps there was an awareness, but no matter. I would do it again if I had the opportunity.

You see, all my son's life I had seen him walk in shame, paying the debt that I had created for him. This at least I could do for him: I could protect him, and hopefully prove that his father was himself forgiven by God for his great sin.

Yes, I jumped forward and threw my arms about Brother Roger. The first stab was nothing, a thud against my breast as if he had clenched a fist and thumped me with it; the second made a huge pain which is with me still, and my left arm was made useless. Still, I could hold on with my right, and this I did. I held him until Bailiff Puttock struck him smartly with the pommel of his sword, and Brother Roger collapsed with me on top of him.

This is the truth, as I believe in the life to come. Oh, Holy Lady, take me and heal me from the sins and pain of this world!

My son, farewell!

Sir Baldwin watched as Brother Humphrey finished the dictation and set the paper aside, snivelling, dropping his reed. The knight's attention went to the frankly bemused expression on the face of the outlaw. Near him lay the knife that had fallen from Brother Roger's hand. Baldwin stared at it a long moment, then at the felon. Slowly, he turned away and faced the group again.

"We must take the body of Brother Peter with us. Perhaps we could put it on the stretcher with the Abbot," he said, walking around the group.

Simon kicked the unconscious Brother Roger. "We have to get this shit back to town as well. And then organize a posse to get the rest of the outlaws."

"They'll be long gone by now," Sir Baldwin said. He looked toward the outlaw. There was a profoundly innocent expression on Hamo's face. "You! Where will your gang be tonight, do you think?"

"They said they were going to head down toward Dartmouth. There're always women to be bought in a sailor's town."

"There you are," Baldwin said. "Now, I know it is not within our jurisdiction to arrest a monk because he falls under Canon Law, but do you think we could tie this fellow and ensure he doesn't try to run away?"

Bailiff Puttock was about to answer when a scrabbling of feet and a gasp made him turn. Where the felon had squatted bound to a tree, there remained only a coil of rope. Hamo was pelting away over the coarse grass.

As the Bailiff made to chase after him, Sir Baldwin put a hand to his arm. "Leave him, friend. There have been enough deaths already. Let's allow one man to remain alive.

"But he and his gang started all this!"

"Yes, I know. But under Canon Law no monk or cleric can be hanged. This man murdered his Abbot, an act of treachery as well as homicide, but can't swing; that felon didn't kill anyone, but he would be hanged as soon as he appeared in a town. Is that justice? Let him go."

The Bailiff watched the man disappear among the thick rocks of the moors. "So long as the damned cretin doesn't fall into another mire again," he said with resignation. "I'll be buggered before I save him a second time!"

THE AMOROUS ARMOURER

When he crouched at the body's side and studied the small, insignificant-looking wound, Sir Baldwin de Furnshill, Keeper of the King's Peace for Crediton in the county of Devonshire, was struck by the melancholy atmosphere of the place.

Often a murder scene felt cold and sad, as if the departing soul had removed all warmth as it fled, but here, in the small hall down an alley off Crediton's high street, there was a sense of poignant gloom that Baldwin had not experienced before, and he looked about him for a moment, wondering where the feeling came from. Certainly it was cold. The fire had been out overnight and there was a damp chill in the air, as though the house had been deserted for months. Apart from that there was little to differentiate the room from many another prosperous artisan's property - nothing except the comparative emptiness.

Usually there would be tapestries, flowers, and occasional scatterings of fresh herbs among the rushes to disguise the distasteful odours where a dog or hog had soiled the floor. Walls would have paintings on them or hangings to keep the cold at bay, tables and cupboards would have good linen spread over them, chairs would have plump cushions – but not here.

Baldwin was honest enough to admit to himself that the decoration was remarkably similar to his own before his marriage. It was unremittingly masculine: there was no indication that it had ever enjoyed the influence of a woman's hand, as if the dead man wanted nothing that might remind him of feminine comforts.

The table tops were plain, scraped wood; stools and benches bare, the fireplace was a rough circle of fire-baked clay on the earthen floor delineated by moorstone rocks. The sole evidence of luxury lay in the man's upper chamber. He had so valued his sleep that he had constructed a bedchamber reached by a ladder.

'You recognize him, Sir Baldwin?'

Baldwin nodded as he reached inside the shirt to study the stab wound more closely. There was a rough oval mark about it, and Baldwin considered it thoughtfully before answering: 'Yes, Tanner. Humphrey the Armourer.'

'He came here little more than a year ago,' Tanner said, his gaze moving about the room. 'Poor bastard.'

Baldwin grunted in agreement. 'No wife?'

'He came here when she died. Some disease or other she got in Exeter.' His tone showed that he was unsurprised by people dying in such a terrible place. Tanner was a heavy man with a square, calm face weather-beaten to a leathery toughness. He always asserted that there were many more vicious and evil creatures in a city like Exeter than in the wilds of Dartmoor.

'And he left behind all his memories,' Baldwin murmured, looking about him once more. It was as if Humphrey had intentionally eradicated all trace of her. Baldwin thought it sad. If his own wife were to die before him, he would want to remember her.

'Some men try to forget dead women,' Tanner suggested. 'Makes it easier to snare another.'

'You think he was a womanizer?'

'Not really. There were rumours he liked the whores, though.'

Baldwin noted that. Any clues might serve to help find the killer. 'Was he robbed?'

'There's a chest up in his bedchamber. His purse is empty.'

Baldwin grunted to himself, then made his way laboriously up the ladder. He had never liked heights, but today the corpse distracted him enough for him to be able to get into the small bedroom before realising how far from the ground he was.

The chamber was large enough for a thick palliasse and chest, which he opened. Inside were clothes and some plate. A thief would have stolen them. There was one other thing Baldwin noticed: by the side of the palliasse was a cloth, a square of fabric with careful embroidery all about the edge. 'A pretty kerchief, Tanner,' he said, letting it fall to the Constable.

Back on solid ground, Baldwin took the kerchief back and smelled it. There was a faint odour of lavender about it. 'Whose was this?' he wondered.

'I've never seen it before,' Tanner said.

'No? It is a distinctive little scrap, though. And out of place in a bachelor's hall. Keep it by, Tanner. We may need it.'

'He won't, will he?' the Constable observed, stuffing it into his belt.

'No, Humphrey is beyond caring. Shame he wasn't wearing some of his armour when this happened,' Baldwin said.

Blood had flowed thinly from the dead man's wound, and there were one or two smudges, as if someone had stood in the gore. Perhaps it was the killer? he mused. No matter. The prints were too indistinct for him to be able to tell anything from them. 'The door was open?'

'No, Sir Baldwin. Locked. We had to come in through the window.'

Baldwin looked up at the unglazed window. It was high in the western wall to catch the dying sun without allowing a thief to clamber in with ease, and now he looked he could see that the timber mullions had been broken. 'You got in there?'

'Yes. But when I got here, there was no key in the door.'

'Where was it?'

'On a ring of keys on his belt. Here.'

Tanner passed him the heavy keyring and Baldwin stood weighing it in his hands. 'You suggest that somebody was in here, stabbed the armourer, left, and the armourer then obligingly rose and locked the door after him? Not with that wound.'

'No,' Tanner agreed. 'He couldn't have got to the door and locked it. He must have died almost immediately.'

'So someone else locked the door, Tanner. From outside, or from in here?'

'There's no other way in or out that I've found.'

'Good! So they left by the door,' Baldwin said. 'And that means that they must have had a key of their own. Who would have been that friendly with this man?'

'That I don't know, Sir Baldwin.'

'Neither do I, so let us speak with the neighbours.'

They were all waiting outside under the suspicious gaze of a watchman who held his wooden staff like a man keen to show his expertise. No one would dare to run away.

Not that there was much point, Baldwin reminded himself. There was nowhere to run to for people whose business and livelihood were tied up with Crediton. However, all the neighbours must be kept until they had been attached – made to pay a surety that guaranteed that they would attend the Justice's court when he next appeared. All of them would be fined anyway, because any man who lived near a murder was taxed for the infringement of the King's Peace, which was why the men shuffled resentfully.

'You have sent for the Coroner?' Baldwin asked Tanner quietly.

'Yes. The messenger left at the same time as the man sent to fetch you.'

'Good. So we need not keep these folk too long, hopefully,' Baldwin said. 'Although the dull-witted fool may take his time.'

'He usually does,' Tanner growled.

Both knew the Coroner. Sir Roger of Gidleigh had been a useful ally in Baldwin's previous investigations, but he had been thrown from his horse earlier in the summer and confined to his bed, a shrunken, twisted reminder of his previous hale and powerful self. In his place had been installed Sir Gilbert of Axminster.

Compared with Sir Roger, Sir Gilbert was a weakly and insipid youth. Sir Gilbert had never taken part in a battle, nor had he earned his rank from proving his honour or courage. No, he had become a knight under the ridiculous law by which any man who owned an estate worth more than £40 each year could be compelled to take up knighthood; it led to cretins like Sir Gilbert wearing the golden spurs, Baldwin thought contemptuously. Feeble-minded doddypolls who were scarcely capable of lacing their enamelled sword-belts. And once knighted, Sir Gilbert's puerile sense of humour and effeminate manner had led to his advancement to Coroner. With a King such as Edward II, who preferred favourites like Piers Gaveston and the appalling Hugh Despenser to his own wife, it was no surprise that men like Sir Gilbert found senior posts.

It hurt Baldwin particularly because he had been a 'Poor Fellow Soldier of Christ and the Temple of Solomon', a Knight Templar, who had risked his life in the hell-hole of Acre in 1291 as that great city fell to the Saracen hordes. The Templars had been honourable, devoted monks who had taken the threefold oaths of poverty, chastity and obedience, and yet they had been slaughtered for personal gain. The French King had coveted their wealth, so he unleashed a storm of impossible accusations against them, having them arrested and then burned at the stake like heretics, all because he wanted their money.

That was the prick that drove Baldwin to investigate crimes: he had been the victim of persecution; he had suffered from the lies of politicians; he knew how difficult it was to deny the claims of bigots. All made him determined to protect others who suffered from injustice.

The memory of his dead friends brought a scowl of disgust to his face; the memory of his comrades' foul deaths made him wear an expression of glowering bitterness which lent his dark features a ferocious air, a fact which was brought home to him when he caught the eye of a young girl, who recoiled as though from a blow.

Abruptly he turned and glanced again at the dead man's hall, trying to drive away the memory of Templars burning in their pyres.

'Looks new still, doesn't it?' Tanner said, following the direction of his look. He was still unused to his Keeper's sudden mood swings, even after six years.

Baldwin grunted assent. The hall shone, showing the gleaming white of fresh limewash. The oak timbers were light-coloured, fresh, and had hardly twisted or cracked yet. It would need a couple of good winters to weather them.

Alongside was the man's place of work, and before talking to the waiting neighbours, Baldwin entered it.

It was a long, low building, as new as the hall. At the far end were the huge hammers which were tripped by cams beneath, driven by the massive wheel outside in the leat. A large anvil sat in the middle of the floor, standing upon a section of tree trunk, and all about were sheets of metal, tools, and at the wall, neatly swept piles of the detritus of the forge: steel shards and metal filings. A box held broken blades, larger offcuts from helmets or plate armour, while at one corner there stood straw dummies with armour bound to them. A trestle contained two helms and various farming implements: scythes, hammers, axes, and blades for wooden shovels.

Everywhere there was the stench of the armourer: the sharp tang of metal and rust, the insidious odour of oil, the brackish, unpleasant scent of the filthy water used to quench the red-hot metal and temper it, but above all there were two smells: the sweetness of the beeswax which was rubbed over the metal while still hot to protect it from rusting, and the noisome stink of animal excrement, almost human in its foul pungency.

'He has a pig?' Baldwin asked. There was no sign of it.

'Everyone has a pig,' came Tanner's laconic reply.

Baldwin nodded as he walked to the corner where the smell came from. 'It is not here now. Where is it?'

'Maybe it's out in the orchard or the woods?'

'Odd time of year for that,' Baldwin said. Hogs were usually left to rootle about in yards on their own, which was why they so often escaped and caused such mayhem in the roads. They were such a nuisance that if someone caught another man's pig, he could demand its execution and claim its trotters as his reward.

He could learn nothing from a pig's excrement. Baldwin peered about him again. It was a remarkably well-ordered smithy. Blacksmiths he had known tended to work bare-chested, apart from their leathery aprons, in black, sooty rooms. They were invariably wiry, lean men, with hands scarred from gripping hot metal, their faces weathered and crazed with wrinkles from staring into white-hot charcoal as they tempered blades and armour. Humphrey's forge was almost clean and tidy by comparison. Only by the anvil itself were there the fine, silvery flakes which showed that red-hot metal had been worked.

It was almost as though the place had been cleaned, ready for his death.

'Massive hammers, those,' Tanner said.

'You need them to make good blades,' Baldwin said, then he paused. 'I wonder if it was one of his own that killed him?'

Back outside, he studied the shuffling, anxious men.

'Who lived nearest the armourer?' Baldwin called out. Although there was a general movement among the men standing before him, no one cared to volunteer information to the Keep of the King's Peace. He was the most powerful and important of all the King's local officials, and as such inspired fear. It was a constant cause of irritation and near-despair for Baldwin. He could never understand why he should be viewed with such alarm. However today he was aware of a certain lethargic dullness growing within him. It was not his place to investigate and report on murders – that was the Coroner's duty – and Baldwin wished to be gone from here. In truth it was tempting to go and leave Sir Gilbert to his task

48

– but if he did, he knew there was a risk that the wrong man could be arrested for the murder. He had no faith in Sir Gilbert.

With a sigh, Baldwin accepted that he must inquire himself, just to ensure that the innocent might walk free.

The crowd was a curious blend of people. Two poor-looking churls, Ham from Efford and Adam Weaver, and one more affluent serf, Jaket the Baker. Ham and Jaket's women clung to their husbands with terror in their eyes, while Adam's wife Edith stood proudly apart. Children mingled with the adults, plainly fretful, and a pair of dogs fought, egged on by two lads with sticks.

Baldwin could smell the fear rising from them like a sour miasma that crept into his nostrils and made him feel tainted. Poor people always stood to lose when they were investigated, he reflected: the rich could afford a pleader to lie for them.

Picking a man at random, he pointed at Ham. 'You! Come here!'

Ham started, nervously smiling, a weasely fellow with a sallow complexion framing sunken dark eyes and pinched cheeks. 'My Lord?'

Baldwin beckoned. Ham had been standing with his wife and two young girls. He left them reluctantly, approaching Baldwin with his eyes downcast.

'You are Ham from Efford, aren't you?' Baldwin demanded. He vaguely remembered that the man had been working with a cloth-maker some while ago.

'Yes, sir.'

'You work with John in …'

'No, he let me go when he took on a new apprentice. An apprentice is cheaper than a trained man.'

Baldwin nodded, and his voice became more gentle. 'Where do you live?'

'In that house,' he pointed. 'My family has a room at the back.'

It was two doors along the alley from the armourer's place. 'How well did you know Humphrey?'

'Hardly at all. He was a cocky bastard, making his bloody metal all day. You could hear the din ten miles off, I reckon.'

This was declared in a wheedling tone, like a beggar whining for alms. Baldwin raised his voice. 'Who else disliked him?' There was no answer and he spoke coldly to Ham. 'Perhaps the dead man was not so troubling to others, eh?'

'They thought the same,' Ham said sulkily. 'Jaket? You had enough trouble with him.'

Baldwin beckoned the man. 'Jaket, what can you tell me about Humphrey's death?'

'Sir Baldwin, I know nothing about his death,' Jaket said. He was a large, pudding-faced man with sparse hair and a large gut. Baldwin recalled seeing him often enough in taverns and inns, always with genially beaming features. Jaket was the first to lead singing or to call for fresh ales, a good companion for an alehouse.

'Did either of you see Humphrey yesterday?' Baldwin asked.

Ham shook his head. 'I was working all day, logging in the Dean's garden.'

Baldwin nodded. He could check with the Dean of Crediton's Collegiate Church later. 'What of you, Jaket?'

'I think I did see him, yes.'

'Where?'

'In the alley, near his door. He was with a tall, foppish young fellow, fair-haired, wearing a rich scarlet tunic. He must have been a knight, from his belt and spurs.'

Baldwin was struck by the similarity between this description and Sir Gilbert. 'Did you hear them talking?'

'I didn't go close to them.'

Ham spoke up. 'He never got on with the armourer. They've been fighting in the courts for ages, ever since Humphrey first came here.'

Baldwin vaguely remembered hearing of their battles in court. 'What was the dispute?'

Jaket had reddened. 'It was nothing much. He built his forge on my land, but when I told him he refused to stop building, said he had bought the land fairly and it was nothing to do with me. I couldn't fight with him, so I paid a lawyer to argue my case in the Church court. Dean Clifford chose to find in favour of Humphrey.'

'And that rankled,' Baldwin observed.

'No. Not much,' Jaket protested.

Baldwin did not believe him. Jaket had realized that admitting to an unneighbourly dispute could make him the most obvious suspect. '"Not much"? Does that mean that you were happy to lose your land? How much did he take?'

'Half the forge is on my land,' Jaket said, throwing a fierce glare at Ham. 'And he never even offered to buy it. How would you feel? Anyway, I didn't talk to them because they were arguing. Something about money.'

'Who else could wish to harm Humphrey?' Baldwin asked.

It was Jaket's turn to implicate someone to deflect attention from himself, and he jerked his chin at Edith Weaver. 'Ask her.'

'Edith?' Baldwin asked with surprise. 'What have you to say for yourself?'

'Nothing, Sir Baldwin,' she said, casting a cold glance at the watchman, who had prodded her forward with the butt of his staff.

She was a comely woman, a brunette of maybe twenty years, of middle height, with an oval face that, although it was not beautiful, had the attractions of youth and energy. Slanting eyes met Baldwin's with resolution, but also a slight anxiety. However Baldwin would not convict anyone for appearing nervous before a King's official.

By comparison, her husband was a pop-eyed fool of some thirty years, with the flabby flesh of the heavy drinker who scarcely bothers with solid food. He had the small eyes of a rat, but set in a pale, round face. Baldwin had never liked him, and liked him even less when he thought of Edith.

'Ask anyone here,' Jaket said. 'She's got a common fame for whoring. She's notorious!'

'Edith?' Baldwin said. 'Have you anything to say?' He could smell lavender again, he thought. It was on the woman. A cheap perfume.

'What can a wife do, when her husband has no work and spends his days in the tavern?'

'Shut up, you stupid bitch!' Adam snarled.

'When did you last bring money for me and our children?'

'I'm going to get work soon.'

'Oh, yes? For six months you've given me nothing for food or drink, but have taken everything you could to fill your guts with ale, you drunken sot! What did you expect me to do? Watch my children starve?' she sneered.

51

Baldwin stared at him coldly. 'Adam, I shall question you in a moment. For now, be silent!' He faced Edith. 'So, you do not deny your trade?'

'Why should I? Don't most wives have to turn to selling their bodies at one time or another?'

Baldwin reflected that his own wife was born to a more fortunate environment. 'Did you see Humphrey yesterday?'

She was quiet for a moment, as if choosing whether to lie, and Baldwin snapped his fingers to Tanner. The Constable pulled the kerchief from his belt and passed it to him.

Adam cried out, 'Edith, your kerchief!'

Baldwin said, 'This was beside his bed. It is yours?'

'Yes, it's mine,' she agreed.

'Where were you last night? Were you there?'

She paused again, but this time Baldwin had noticed something else. 'What is that?' he asked, pointing at her foot.

On one sole of her thin sandals he had seen a mark, and there was a corresponding smudge on the inner side of her foot below her ankle. Edith gazed down at it with a kind of weary resignation.

'It is blood, is it not?' Baldwin said sternly.

She sighed and nodded. 'Yes. I had to flee after I saw him die. Humphrey was here in the yard yesterday morning, and he asked me to visit him last night. I knew Adam would be in the tavern till late, so he wouldn't care, and Humphrey always paid me well, so I agreed.'

'When were you to go to him?'

'At dusk. But when I arrived, he was in the forge talking to the man Jaket described. I walked into the hall and drank some of his wine. When I heard him leaving the forge and talking outside, I went up the ladder to his chamber and began to doff my clothes. He was talking angrily, I thought. I wasn't sure if he would still want me, but I was desperate for the money, so I prepared. My kerchief and skirts were already off when I heard him come in, and a gust blew out the candles. I could see nothing in the dark. I took off my other garments, thinking he would soon join me, and then … I heard it.'

She lifted her eyes to meet Baldwin's serious gaze. 'It was like the thud of a clod of soil thrown at a man's back. I heard Humphrey curse, then cough, and I heard him say, "You have killed me!" and there was a tumbling noise, then a rough, rattling sound, as of a man with too much phlegm in his throat. I remained silent up in the chamber, not daring to move, until I heard the door slam. Then I donned my clothing as speedily as I might, and rushed down the ladder to him, but I was too late.'

'He was dead?'

'Yes. There was nothing I could do. And I feared that if I called the Constable, I would be suspected. What else could I do? I ran.'

'The door was locked,' Baldwin said.

'I locked it.'

'Where did you get the key?'

'He always kept a spare in the forge, hanging with his tools. Everyone knew about it. I went there to fetch it, locked the house, and returned the key to the forge. I was scared – but I am no murderer.'

Which explained why the hall was locked but the forge open, Baldwin thought. 'Did you see whom it was that entered the hall with Humphrey and stabbed him?'

'No. I swear it.'

Jaket interrupted eagerly. 'Surely it was the tall knight I saw with Humphrey earlier.' And then his eyes widened with horror.

'Perhaps,' Baldwin said. 'But there is no proof of that.'

'Proof of what, Sir Baldwin? My Heavens, have you decided to hold the inquest without me? Eh? Won't do, Sir Baldwin. No, it won't!'

Sir Gilbert, Sir Baldwin sourly told himself, could scarcely have picked a better time to have arrived.

Baldwin sent Tanner to fetch bread, wine and some roasted meats, then joined Sir Gilbert in the hall. They sat at Humphrey's table, and while they waited for their meal to arrive, Baldwin summarised the evidence he had heard so far.

Sir Gilbert appeared unconcerned by Humphrey's death. 'He wasn't a terribly good metalsmith.'

'But you chose to buy from him.'

'I didn't know how poor his work was. Not that it matters. I have an almost complete suit of armour and have paid nothing.'

'How so?' Baldwin asked in surprise.

'I was here to collect it yesterday, but the helm didn't fit snugly. It was shoddy, quite shoddy, so I told him to fix it before I would pay him anything. He wasn't happy, of course, but then, who ever is? Serfs nowadays are so surly. They hardly even show the manners they were born with.' He yawned, adding petulantly, 'Where's that damned fool with the food?'

'He will not be long,' Baldwin said. 'What time did you leave Humphrey yesterday?'

Sir Gilbert had curious eyes that remained half-lidded, as though he was in a perpetual state of confused lethargy. It was one of the reasons why Sir Baldwin disliked him, but now he also found himself distrusting the knight as well.

'Are you suggesting that I could have had any part in his death, Sir Baldwin?'

'I said no such thing. I merely inquired when you left Crediton yesterday.'

'I should take it very ill, should you accuse me of murder, Sir Baldwin.'

Baldwin leaned back and stared unblinkingly at Sir Gilbert, his left hand on the table top, his right near his belt where he could reach his small riding sword. 'If I were to accuse, I would be happy to allow you trial by combat, Sir Gilbert.'

Sir Gilbert chuckled. 'I think you would find the combat rather short, and I would find it not to my liking,' he said frankly.

Tanner entered with a pair of cooks, and soon Baldwin and Sir Gilbert were tucking into their food. As they ate, Baldwin admired the small dagger which Sir Gilbert used to cut his food.

'This knife? I bought it from the armourer,' Sir Gilbert said when asked.

When they were finished, Baldwin asked, 'What time did you leave? After all, your servants can confirm when you did go.'

That was no threat. Any knight could guarantee his own servants would perjure themselves to support their master.

Sir Gilbert sipped wine from his mazer and then steepled his fingers under his nose. 'I see no reason not to answer you. I left almost immediately after seeing my armour. It was quite late.'

'You had angry words with him outside the forge?'

Sir Gilbert's eyes widened marginally. 'Who told you of that?'

'A witness.'

'Let us say, he was not happy that he would have to wait for payment.'

'Not happy enough to come to blows?'

'You overstep your mark, Sir Baldwin,' Sir Gilbert grated.

'And I would hear your answer.'

'However I would not answer impertinence,' he snapped. 'Now, if you have no objection, Sir Baldwin, I wish to conduct my official enquiry.'

Baldwin stood behind the Coroner as the town's jury shuffled in. Every man from the age of twelve was brought inside and stood nervously at the wall, their eyes reflecting their consciousness of the seriousness of the matter. A cleric from the Church had already taken up his post at Sir Gilbert's side, reed in hand, to record the inquest. That was the Coroner's first duty, after all, to record all the facts about a murder so that the justices could try the murderer later.

Adam, Ham and Jaket were led in, Edith at their rear. The four were taken to a point between the jury and Sir Gilbert, who sat on a low seat and studied them.

'Sir Baldwin de Furnshill has informed me of your evidence,' he began. 'First, Jury, you must agree how this man died.'

He walked to the body and stripped it naked, with Tanner's help. 'See? One stab in the chest, by a blade probably an inch broad at the hilt. It reaches in,' he added, shoving his forefinger into the hole, 'Not more than about four inches. I think it's fair to say that he died almost instantly: it went straight to his heart.'

Rolling the body over and over, he showed that the corpse had no other wounds.

Tanner glanced at Baldwin. 'Sir, there are no cuts on his hands.'

'No,' Sir Gilbert said sharply, drawing Tanner's attention back to him. 'So we can assume that this murderous attack happened swiftly, before he could think of protecting himself. He didn't have time to grab the blade and push it away.'

He turned from the body and returned to his seat. 'The question is, who amongst you could have so hated this man that you killed him? My first thought is you, Adam.'

'Me?' The squeal was like that of a pig, Baldwin thought, and with that thought, he wondered again about the excrement in the forge.

'Yes, you! You knew that your wife was whoring about the place, didn't you? You knew that Humphrey was enjoying her, didn't you?'

'No, no, I didn't!'

'You didn't know your wife was selling her body?'

'Well ... I knew that, yes.'

'So you took your revenge on him.'

Adam shivered slightly. 'I'd have beaten her if I'd guessed she was lying with a neighbour, yes, but not him.'

'You expect me to believe that?'

'We needed the money,' Adam said simply.

'You mean,' Sir Gilbert's voice reflected his disbelief, 'you mean you'd happily allow her to whore her way around the town so long as she didn't sleep with a near neighbour?'

'It'd be hard to look a neighbour in the face if she had,' Adam said apologetically. 'I'll thrash her for that later.'

Baldwin had to control a chuckle. Sir Gilbert was being confronted with a different set of rules and principles of honour. To have one's wife lie with other men was all right, but not if her clients were close neighbours! But then the thought of the pig returned to him, and he watched the men with interest.

'Jaket, you must have detested this man because of your litigation against him.'

'Oh, you expect that kind of problem,' Jaket said off-handedly. 'It's not as if it was a huge dispute.'

'It went to court! You had to pay pleaders!'

Jaket licked his dry lips and tried to wear a smile. 'The money the lawyer charged cannot be laid at Humphrey's door. I knew how much they could cost before I started the case.'

'And he won the matter, keeping the forge on your land.'

Jaket shrugged. 'It happens.'

Sir Gilbert pressed him. 'Weren't you angry? Didn't you complain about the noise?'

'I don't deny that. Almost everyone in the alley complained about it. They shook the foundations of all our places, those hammers, and the smoke! You should have seen this alley on a windless day. Smoke and fumes all over. You couldn't hardly breathe!'

'Sir Gilbert, may I ask a question?' Baldwin enquired.

He was rewarded with an expression of annoyance, but then the knight gave him a dismissive wave of the hand, as if Sir Gilbert was indulging him. 'Please do, Sir Baldwin,' he said.

'Thank you. Jaket, do you have a pig?'

'Yes. It's in the orchard.'

'Did Humphrey keep a pig?'

'No, he didn't have space for one.'

'And yet his forge has sheltered one. Whose would that have been?'

'Ham's. His hog went wandering a couple of days ago and Humphrey managed to catch it.'

'Ham? Is this true?' Baldwin asked.

'Um. Yes.' Ham had his fingers intertwined, and he twisted them as he tried to meet Baldwin's eye.

'Did he demand the trotters?'

Ham suddenly flinched as though someone had struck him. 'It wasn't fair! The pig is all we have left! Since I lost my work, I've had nothing, but what I could afford, I've shoved into the pig to fatten him, so that come winter there'd be enough for us to eat, and then Humphrey, God rot his balls, comes and tells me he's taken my hog and stuck it in his forge, and unless I agree to have it killed and give him the trotters, he'll keep it. I couldn't let him do that.'

'So instead you went to him, stabbed him, and rescued your hog,' Sir Gilbert said scathingly. 'How much fairer and more just.'

'No, I didn't! I went to his house to try to argue with him as darkness was falling, but the door was locked and he wouldn't answer it, not matter how hard I banged on it. And then I heard my pig, and I thought, well, if he's not there, I could at least get my pig back. But I didn't even have to break down the door because it was open already. I fetched my pig and took him home.'

'You expect us to believe this?' Sir Gilbert demanded. 'Pathetic! It's the most unbelievable tale I have heard in many years!'

'I swear it's true, Sir.'

'You had the motive and you had the means,' Sir Gilbert said gleefully, pointing at Ham's belt. 'Your knife!'

Ham reluctantly pulled it from its sheath and passed it to him, and Baldwin studied it. 'No blood,' he said, and held it up for all to see. 'And the blade is a good nine inches long.'

'So?' Sir Gilbert asked.

'So it was not used to kill Humphrey. There is one additional point about the deadly stab wound,' Baldwin continued, walking to the corpse and pointing. 'About it there is a ring-like bruise. I think it means the killer stabbed with main force, driving the blade in sharply as far as he could. The hilt struck Humphrey's flesh, and marked it in this manner.'

'And what does that tell us?' Sir Gilbert asked suavely.

'That the handle struck him, which means that a long blade like this would probably have gone right through him,' Baldwin explained.

'It might not,' Sir Gilbert said. 'It could have struck his shoulder bone and thus not penetrated his back.'

'If that were the case, the hilt would not have struck his chest,' Baldwin pointed out. 'No, Humphrey was killed with a shorter blade.'

'Who has a shorter blade?'

'Sir Gilbert, you have a shorter blade, do you not?' Baldwin said mildly, pointing to the knife on his belt.

Sir Gilbert was suddenly very still. 'You accuse me?'

'I do not accuse any man,' Baldwin said pointedly. 'I only wish to get to the truth. I would like to call another witness. Do you object?'

'I ...' Sir Gilbert was white-faced with rage, but seeing the interested attention of the whole jury, and the reed poised over the paper in the clerk's hand, he swallowed his ire with difficulty. 'Call whomever you wish,' he rasped finally.

'Let us hear your servant,' Baldwin continued, and when the man had been brought in, Baldwin made him stand before the jury, his back to his master.

'I want to ask you about last night,' he said.

'Sir.'

'Were you with your master?'

'Yes, sir.'

'From dusk?'

'Well, all afternoon, sir.'

'So you were with him here, when he came to see Humphrey?'

'I was holding his horse for him at the entrance to the alley.'

'I see. When your master appeared, how was he?'

'He was angry, sir.'

'Because the armour was no good?'

'Not only that ...'

'Why, then?'

The servant tried to turn to look at his master, but Baldwin brought his hand down heavily on his shoulder. 'Answer!'

'Because he'd made an offer for the man's woman, so Humphrey grew wrathful with my master.'

Baldwin looked at Sir Gilbert. He appeared almost to have fallen asleep. 'Your master offered Humphrey money for his woman?'

'Yes, but Humphrey said he wouldn't accept all the gold in the Pope's palace at Avignon for her.'

'Did your master have blood on his tunic?'

'He was wearing his scarlet tunic, Sir Baldwin.'

'The perfect clothing for murder,' Baldwin observed.

'I killed no one,' Sir Gilbert snapped.

'Then who killed Humphrey?' Baldwin said.

'The girl said that the candles were out. I left before the full dark. If I'd been there, she would have seen me,' Sir Gilbert protested.

'Did Ham collect his pig after Humphrey's death? The house was locked,' Baldwin mused. 'Was it full dark, then, Ham?'

'No, it was as the light was fading. It was dull, but not dark yet.'

Baldwin glanced up at the west-facing window, puzzled. 'How long was your master gone?'

Sir Gilbert's man considered. 'Not long. I could hear them. Then Sir Gilbert came hurrying. He jumped on his horse and spurred away, and I had to hurry to mount my pony and ride off to catch up. As I left Crediton, all I could see was the fading sun catching his harness in the distance.'

'So it was not full dark even then?' Baldwin said.

'No, sir.'

Baldwin faced Sir Gilbert. 'And you had not paid this armourer, you told me?'

'I refused to pay him until my helm was ready. Would you have done?'

Baldwin ignored his question, instead turning to face the four suspects again. 'This murder was committed by someone who was well known by Humphrey. That was how the killer got so close to him.'

'A thief might have waylaid him,' Sir Gilbert said.

'Behind what would the thief have lain hidden? Humphrey was killed in the open, there, in the middle of his floor. No, he was with someone he knew. He didn't expect to be murdered. He thought he was safe.'

Baldwin stood still, contemplatively staring up at the window.

'The trouble is, so many of his neighbours disliked him. But they could have killed him at any time. They had no reason to kill him last night. Only one person could have wished to kill him last night, and only one could have got close enough.'

'Do you accuse me?' Sir Gilbert said, his voice low and dangerous.

'Sir Gilbert, please calm yourself. I know you are only recently dubbed knight, but it is not chivalrous to lose your temper,' Sir Baldwin said, and as Sir Gilbert swelled as though about to explode, he continued, 'No, it was the Coroner's argument with the armourer which points us to the murderer. The Coroner wanted to offer money for the woman he had seen going to warm Humphrey's bed, and that enraged Humphrey.'

'He didn't attack me, if that's what you're leading up to,' Sir Gilbert snapped.

'No. He went inside and spoke to his whore, an attractive young woman for whom he felt a very affection. Him, a man whose wife had died some while before, a lonely man living almost in a barn. Look at this place, you can see, you can feel his desperate loneliness! What more natural than that he should want a woman to share this with him? And what could be more natural than that he should want the woman who so regularly comforted him to share his life?'

'I couldn't do that, sir,' Edith said modestly. 'I am already married.'

'We all know of women who can and do leave their husbands,' Baldwin said gently, 'and a man in love may even think of disposing of a rival. Did he suggest that to you?'

'Me, sir? Why should he do that, sir?'

'Because he loved you, Edith. And he probably thought that you loved him too, which was why he didn't think you would mind when he told you he could not pay you.'

'Of course he could pay me,' she said, but her face had paled.

'No. He had nothing in his purse. There was plate in his chest, which a robber would have taken, but he had no money. Perhaps he was relying upon Sir Gilbert's cash to pay you.'

'No! I couldn't have hurt him!'

'You say it was dark, but all the others were here at dusk. Ham was here after the murder, if your story is true and you locked the door before going. Before that, Jaket saw Sir Gilbert here. Sir Gilbert left without entering the hall. But you were here.'

'He threatened me, sir, what could I do?' she said, throwing caution to the winds and falling to her knees at his feet. 'He wanted me to leave Adam and live with him, wanted me without paying. I couldn't do that! I was bound to Adam by my vows. I had to draw my knife in defence!'

'He thought you loved him. He thought you would willingly agree to sleep with him for free. And you stabbed him to death.'

'He was killed because I didn't pay for my armour?' Sir Gilbert said, shocked.

'Edith needed the cash. He made his use of her, but then failed to reimburse her. In a rage, she lashed out with her little dagger.'

Sir Gilbert glanced at her belt and saw her delicate knife. 'Which is too short to penetrate both sides of his body.'

'But long enough to puncture his heart,' Baldwin agreed.

Sir Gilbert motioned to the clerk at his side. 'Record that the woman Edith has confessed her guilt.'

Edith stood up and allowed herself to be gripped by Tanner. Baldwin took her dagger and studied it. 'Blood,' he said, tossing it to Sir Gilbert.

'I do not understand how you decided that it was her and not one of the other people,' Sir Gilbert said, pouring wine.

Having completed the public aspects of the inquiry, now the two sat at the table once more, having supervised the removal of the body, while the clerk took an inventory of the dead man's belongings.

'It did not make sense to me,' Baldwin explained. 'Why should any of his neighbours suddenly decide to kill him? Surely there must be a striking event which gave someone cause to murder him yesterday?'

'The pig?'

'I thought of that, but Humphrey had taken his pig. You can be assured that Humphrey would not have let Ham get too close to him. If Ham had been there, Humphrey would have had defensive wounds on his hands and arms, as he would if it was Jaket or Adam. He would be on his guard with any of them. As he would have been with you. Especially since you had refused to pay him. No, that did not seem credible. But the thought led me to think that of all people, a man is at his most defenceless with women. The argument with you about his woman left him furious, and perhaps he was more determined than ever to rescue her from the degrading life of a whore.'

'And she turned upon him.'

'How else would a whore respond? He had tried to persuade her of his love as soon as you left – when Ham came, it was still dusk, and Humphrey was already dead, so he had had no time to bed her. But she assumed he was trying to avoid paying her. In a rage, she stabbed. Maybe she only meant to hurt him, to show that she was not so foolish as to be taken in.'

'Why did she leave her kerchief behind?'

'Now you test me,' Baldwin said. 'It was beside the bed, so I think she agreed to let him keep it as a memento some time ago. Perhaps she thought it would be a good way to keep her client bound to her. He would have something to remember her by, even when she was not with him.'

'Why did she lock the door and go through that charade of leaving the forge open?'

'Panic. Her first instinct was to bolt, but then she thought that anyone could walk in, and too many knew she had been there. Better if she leave the body hidden for a while.'

'But left the key in the forge where anyone could get it.'

'That was clever. If anyone could get it, anyone could have killed him.'

'She is plainly a dangerous woman.'

'Yes,' Baldwin said, his gaze travelling about the room once more. His voice fell, and he spoke as if to himself. 'But only to sad, lonely men who thought her body could be taken as a gift, when it was merely a commodity she traded for money. That is the sadness. That Humphrey truly loved her. Did you see how similar her knife was to yours?'

'They could have been twins.'

'Yes. She told me that he gave it to her. It was a gift.'

He glanced at the window once more, and shivered.

'Can you imagine how he felt? A lonely man, missing his first wife, who at last declared his love for another woman, only to be stabbed with the very token of love he had given her. It's no wonder he didn't protect himself. He probably did not want to.'

A CLERICAL ERROR

He had broken the law, and right this minute, that was all John Mattheu, novice at the Abbey of Tavistock in Devonshire, in the year of Grace thirteen hundred and twenty two, could think of. It saved him from considering the body in the stream before him.

Why had he come here? Every day he exercised the Abbot's horses, but rarely this way. He could only assume an evil spirit had guided him. If only someone else had found him. Anyone else.

It was the dogs that brought him to his senses again. They were all over the place, panting in the unusually warm weather. Brother Peter the almoner had told him with a dry chuckle only yesterday that any weather other than rain was unseasonal on Dartmoor, and John had to agree. Since he had arrived at Tavistock two years ago, he had endured more dampness than he would have thought possible.

That it was a man was obvious from the boots and the outline of the strong shoulders under the black woollen cloak. His tippet was thrown up over his head concealing his features, and it had soaked up water from the little brook into which the man had fallen. At his side a scruffy mastiff stared down at the man forlornly. The brute looked familiar, but John couldn't remember where he'd seen it before; so many people had dogs for their protection, and right now it was the long-legged hunting raches of his Abbot's which demanded his attention.

He had broken the law. If he weren't on the moors illegally, he could have ridden back to town, raised the hue and cry, and told the Abbot, but the rolling, grassy and rock-scattered moors were legally forest, hunting grounds owned by the King, and bringing hounds here was a serious offence that could cost the abbey dearly. The Sheriff would not be impressed, nor would the Coroner. And Abbot Champeaux had not given permission for John to bring the dogs. Whichever way he looked at it, John was in trouble.

What should he do? He tentatively reached down to the body, curling his lip as he felt the soggy shoulder of the woollen cloak, tugging it away, and then gasped with shock, for he knew the man: Ralph atte Moor, one of the King's own Foresters.

'Oh! Dear God!' he moaned. 'Why me?'

*

His journey back to the abbey was a great deal swifter than his casual ride out, and his mind was churning with near panic as he clattered in through the water gate to the court behind, hurling himself from the saddle and landing on the forepaw of one of the bitches, making her yelp with hurt surprise.

'Hey, there, boy! Ware the beasts!' roared a voice, and John looked up to see the grim features of Peter the almoner staring down at him.

Peter was a fearsome looking man. His face was badly scarred by a hideous axe wound that stretched along the line of his jaw from the point of his chin to below his ear. Novices whispered that he had gained it during one of the raids by the Scots, when their false King Robert Bruce had attacked as far as Carlisle, slaughtering and burning as he went. Peter had been a brother in one of the priories put to the torch, and the murderous villains had tried to kill him along with his brethren, but the blow intended to decapitate him had merely shattered his jaw and stunned him. Later he had come to, and a physician in Carlisle had somehow saved his life.

His pate never needed shaving. Although he had the bushiest eyebrows John had ever seen, and his reddish hair showed little sign of greying, there was little left of it, only a fringe that began at one temple and reached around the back of his skull to the other. When the barber came, he only ever asked for a few ounces of blood to be taken, and swore that the cause of his long life was that simple precaution.

Now the fifty-year-old monk was gazing down at him with exasperation in his grey eyes. 'Well? What on God's good, green earth, is so important that you should leap on to the lord Abbot's raches?'

'He's dead! I found him out on the moor, and . . .'

'Quietly boy! Calm yourself!' Peter scowled at him thoughtfully, then took him by the elbow and led him into the gatehouse. There was a great earthenware jug resting by the fire, and he filled a mazer and handed it to John. 'Drink this.'

The strong, heavily spiced wine warmed his belly and sent shoots of fire to his toes. 'Ralph atte Moor, sir. I found him in the stream by the quarries near Dennithorne. He's dead.'

'What were you doing up there?'

John flushed. 'Exercising the Abbot's horse and hounds.'

'The raches don't need to go on the moors for their exercise,' Peter observed drily. 'No matter. The body is more important. Let me answer for the dogs.'

He sat staring at the fire while John finished his drink, and John knew what was uppermost in his mind. Ralph was unpopular with everyone. Harsh in language, brutal with those who infringed Forest Law, he was a bully with the power to gaol people. He would strike a man down for any supposed misdemeanour. John knew of Ralph, although Peter knew him better. Peter had the duty of distributing charity to the people at the Abbey's gates and supplying the lepers at the Maudlin, so he could often visit the town's taverns. It made Peter a useful source of local gossip for other monks.

'His dog was there?' Peter asked.

'Yes, sir.'

'He is a big bugger, that mastiff,' Peter mused. 'Was there any sign who could have killed Ralph?'

'Nothing I could see, sir.'

'Probably because like all youngsters, you don't have eyes in your head for anything other than women and the nearest wine flagon, eh? Fortunately, I am more observant. Well, I suppose we should tell the Abbot and get up there. Come along, boy!'

The Abbot did not see John personally, but Peter made it clear that their lord was not pleased with him. John must exercise the hounds, but that didn't mean he had permission to go on the moors, where even the Abbot was not permitted. The Abbot had himself been rebuked for chasing deer on the moors occasionally, but for a novice to take it into his head to do the same was a different matter.

Reeve Miria was informed, and he arrived on his horse through the court gate within the hour. Robert Miria was a squat, fair haired man with a face like a walnut, dark and wrinkled. His expression was sour. 'What's all this then? I hear Ralph's dead. That right?'

'Aye.' Peter led the way through the water gate, over the bridge, through the deerpark, then up the hill to the moor. It took little time for him to explain what had happened. 'Since there were no vicious marauders there, it seemed pointless to raise the shire's militia.'

'Don't be sarcastic, old goat! I'll decide whether to raise the Hue when I get back.'

Peter shrugged, loping along easily. His pace was clearly comfortable for him, although John found himself growing tired. He had suggested that they should have horses saddled and bridled, but Peter had looked at him from his bushy eyebrows and growled that God gave man legs to use, and horses were only for the vain.

'Can't you move faster?' the Reeve demanded again as John lagged behind.

John had not enough energy to respond. It was all he could manage just to keep his legs moving.

At the quarry the two men waited for John, Robert Miria gulping from a wineskin while Peter refreshed himself with a few sips from the stream, drinking from a cupped hand.

Even over his exhaustion, after climbing for at least a mile and a half, John could see that the old monk was alert. He bent one knee at the side of the stream, one hand on the ground, the other in the water, then lifted it swiftly, his eyes ranging over the horizon ahead in case a gang of felons might attempt to attack. John had the impression of strength and power, like a man who could spring up in a moment to defend himself.

Joan sank down at the water's side and thrust his face into the stream, drinking deeply.

'How much farther, boy?' Peter asked.

'A half mile, perhaps.'

'Come on, then,' Reeve Miria said. 'I have other matters to deal with at Tavistock.'

'You always were a busy man,' Peter said, scanning the land ahead.

'A merchant needs to be busy. It's people like me who keep the town alive. Without burgesses, there's be nothing. And that would mean nothing to keep you lot in the abbey alive either!'

'Oh, I think we could survive,' Peter responded, checking his sandals. 'Our manors would keep us going. It's not as though the town shares all its profits with us.'

'The abbey gets the rents,' the Reeve snarled. 'And extortionate they can be, too.'

'But they are not usury,' Peter said.

The Reeve stared at Peter as the monk carried on. 'What's that supposed to mean?'

'Nothing. I'd heard that someone was charging interest on money loaned, that's all. Illegal, of course, but some folk will try to make money they don't need. It's as bad as a doctor charging money from a poor man: the doctor should value life more highly than money. God in his goodness gave the doctor the skills necessary to save life, so the doctor is charging for God's gift of knowledge - it's obscene! Therefore a merchant shouldn't ask profit from lending money. If he has money to lend, he must have sufficient already; only a thief would demand profit from lending it.'

'You're talking crap!'

'Christ's teaching?' Peter asked with apparent interest. His lisp, caused by the crushing of his jaw and the loss of almost all the teeth on one side of his mouth, sounded almost like a laugh, and John wondered what the point of the conversation was. He was convinced that Peter wouldn't have raised the matter had there not been a reason.

'Come on, I don't have time for all this shit!' the Reeve said dismissively.

'Of course. Oh, I should warn you: I asked Ivo Colbrok and Eustace Joce to meet us up near the place.'

'Why?'

'Oh, I just have a feeling that they might be able to help,' Peter said, setting off again.

He was right. At the entrance to Dennithorne a small group had gathered. The men John recognised: Eustace Joce, the tenant who farmed Dennithorne, and Ivo Colbrok, who looked after the Abbot's warrens in Dolvin Wood. There was also a woman, whom John did not recognise, but whom he thought must be Eustace's wife, from the familiarity with which he treated her.

Peter stood among the group, looking at them all. 'Lordings, I am sorry to have asked you to meet us here, but we have a solemn duty. A man's body has been found, and we must report on it for the Coroner when he arrives.'

'D'you know who it is?' Eustace asked. He was a large, leathery skinned man, dressed in a strong rather than fine linen shirt, with a leather jacket atop. His massive biceps were as thick as a maid's waist, John thought.

'Ralph atte Moor.'

Eustace Joce said nothing, but looked at the woman, who had given a startled cry and her hand went to her face on hearing the name. 'Not poor Ralph?'

Peter's voice became more gentle as he said, 'I am afraid so, maid. He is a little way further up here.'

She shook her head and tears began to run slowly down her cheeks.

'Typical of the fool. Dry your eyes, Anastasia! Anyone would think he was close to you, eh?' Eustace watched his wife with small, suspicious eyes.

'It's only right that a man should be mourned,' Peter said quietly.

'I don't see why. A fool like him doesn't deserve compassion. He was a shit when he lived, and I don't give a fig what anyone else says.'

'That is not a very compassionate attitude,' Peter remonstrated.

'He made one enemy too many,' Eustace said harshly as he set his face to the hill.

'Was he unpopular, would you say?' Peter asked.

'You know damn well he was!'

'Ah!' Peter said mildly, and Eustace shot him a questioning look, but Peter merely trudged on thoughtfully and didn't speak again until they were at the body.

*

Ralph had a great swelling on his forehead when they pulled him out of the water in which he lay face-down.

'Perhaps he simply drowned?' Peter murmured, and asked John to help him roll the body over. When John saw Ralph's face, although he had helped lay out two monks and one lay brother, he felt a deep sadness. It was the sympathetic instinct of one man upon seeing how another had died.

Against the pallor of his face, the ugly, blue mark stood out like mark of the devil, and all the gathering stood studying it in silence for some little time.

It was Peter who voiced their thoughts. 'It, um, looks as though he was struck down.'

Nobody spoke. There was a curious atmosphere which John did not fully understand, as though all the men and the woman were waiting for someone else to say something. Peter was the only person who appeared unconcerned. He stood with his left hand cupping his hideously damaged jaw, his elbow supported by his right hand, a vague smile on his twisted face as he looked down at Ralph. 'It would have been a heavy blow,' he said.

'To knock that bastard down, it'd have to be,' Ivo Colbrok said.

Peter sighed to himself and walked to the mastiff. 'Hello, Rumon, old fellow.'

The mastiff was apparently aware that his master was beyond help, and somewhere deep in his canine brain there was an understanding that these people were not here to harm his master, but to help if they may. Unlike most mastiffs, he did not threaten the folks about Ralph's body, but sat back and watched with mournful brown eyes. When Peter went to him, the great head turned to him, but listlessly, as though the reason for his existence was ended.

'Why did you ask us to come to this God-forsaken place?' Ivo demanded, looking from Peter to the Reeve. 'What good can we do here?'

Reeve Miria was watching Peter, who stood patting the dog's head. 'We have to record what is here for the Coroner.'

Eustace sniffed. 'The Coroner won't be pleased if we've messed the whole area about before he can come here.'

'By the time Coroner Roger of Gidleigh can get here,' Peter declared, 'the body will have been eaten and rotted. I am happy to take responsibility for the corpse, but I must see how the land lay so that I can describe it to the Coroner. And then I and my novice here will mount guard until Coroner Roger arrives.'

John thought that his words made good sense. He watched as Peter walked to the stream and stood gazing down. The waters flowed swiftly here, in a steep-sided and moorstone-lined cleft some three feet deep. Above was a stone clapper bridge, formed of a single flat stone that traversed the stream. It was not broad enough for a cart, but few carts travelled up here. This bridge had been thrown over the stream by the miners, who regularly sent their ponies down to Tavistock to replenish their stores, and it was only some two feet wide. Peter stood on it, bouncing himself up and down a little. 'It's solid,' he said. 'It didn't topple and knock him into the water.'

'Of course it didn't!' Reeve Miria said scornfully. 'Since when did a moorstone block that size move.'

'You haven't told us what you want us here for,' Ivo said shrewdly. 'If you wanted only those who were nearest to the body, you'd not have called me up here, you'd just demand Eustace and some of the other locals. The Coroner's rules demand that the people who are nearest and those who're within the parish should be called to view the body. Yet I am a member of Tavistock's parish, while Eustace is a moorman and comes from Lydford parish. Why?'

He was demanding an answer from the Reeve, but the Reeve himself did not answer. Instead he looked over to Peter, who was now kneeling at the side of the stream, between the corpse and the waters. Hearing the question, he looked up. 'You ask why?' he enquired. There was a faint tone of surprise in his voice. 'I should have thought that was obvious, my friend. Because here among us is the killer. All of you had a desire to kill Ralph.'

*

There was a grim silence in answer to his words. John felt anxious, aware that his stomach suddenly felt empty. Peter was staring up at the horizon again, seemingly unaware of the upset and annoyance he had caused.

It was curious that nobody questioned his statement. There was a strange stillness, as though all the people there were holding their breath and waiting for him to make another comment, and John wondered for a moment whether Peter was half expecting an outburst, something that might make the murderer declaim his innocence before all. Eventually, Peter dropped his head and turned to face them.

'Ralph died, I think, either from the blow to his head, or from drowning because he had been stunned and could not lift his mouth and nose above the waters. I can't say that I am expert enough to interpret the signs, but I can be sure that he died some hours ago. He is quite chill, isn't he? That means that he died hours ago and it's taken this long for the warmth to flee his body.'

Ivo Colbrok gave a great 'Hah!' and smiled triumphantly. 'Well that means I could have had nothing to do with his death: I was in the Plymouth Inn last night, and stayed there until this morning, when I went home.'

Peter gave him a shocked look. 'I trust you didn't think I meant you'd killed him, Ivo? The only argument you had with Ralph was about the rabbits.'

'Yes . . . Well . . . He would complain about them every few days. Insisted that my rabbits chewed into his crops last year. Absolute crap, of course. I look after my rabbits, I do. There's no need for them to wander, and why he should think that they'd eat his manky peas and beans, I don't know. Anyway, there was nothing the bastard could do about it,' he added smugly, 'since your Abbot is the owner of the warrens. I pay him rent each year to farm his rabbits, but they are still his own and, as I told Ralph, if he had a problem with them, he should go to the Abbot.'

'Yes,' Peter said ruminatively. His chin was cushioned in his hand again. It was a familiar posture, and John had often wondered whether it was an affectation which he used to conceal his scar. 'The Abbot told me of that. In fact before I came up here today, the Abbot told me to ask you about the argument you had with Ralph last midday.'

Ivo paled and his voice grew quieter. 'I hadn't realised the good Abbot had heard.'

'Oh, the Abbot has good hearing regarding matters which may need to be decided before his court,' Peter said cheerily. 'I understand that it was some other problem?'

'He accused me of trying to poison his dog,' Ivo snarled. 'That monster there! Rumon, he called it, after the saint, which is blasphemy in any man's language.'

Peter smiled at the mastiff, who chose this moment to scratch laboriously at his pendulous jowls, flicking a thick gobbet of saliva some yards, narrowly missing John. 'St Rumon may be the saint most honoured in our church, but Ralph always said that it was only fair that the fellow should be given the saint's name, since he was born on the saint's day.'

'I didn't try to poison the tawny brute, anyway. That was a lie put about by Ralph to justify trying to thump me.'

'I wasn't aware that Ralph required provocation to hit people,' Peter said mildly.

John had noticed before that the almoner tended to avoid a man's eyes when he was questioning them. It was a trait which he had exhibited on occasions with the novices, when he suspected that one was guilty of a misdemeanour, as though by looking away he could hear the truth more distinctly. Only when he was certain of his judgement did he look up and meet his victim's gaze with a firm and determined scowl.

He looked up now, and fixed his stern features on Ivo with the result that Ivo flushed and looked away as though ashamed.

'Did you try to poison his dog?'

Ivo threw his hands out in a gesture of appeal. 'What would you do? The brute got in among my warren. He loved chasing the rabbits, and it was doing none of them any good.'

'So you did?' Peter said sadly, ruffling the dog's ear.

'I would have been justified if I had,' Ivo said evasively.

'You say that you have witnesses last night who can confirm you were at the inn?'

'Yes.'

'What of when they were asleep?'

'The door was bolted.'

'So that it could have been opened from somebody inside?'

'Are you saying I killed him?'

'It's possible. I know you and he had regular arguments.'

'That's rubbish!'

'Perhaps. But, you see, this man's body is very cold. What if he died, let us suppose, early yesterday afternoon?'

'I was at the market.'

'Ah, that's good!' Peter said with simulated relief. 'So you can provide witnesses who saw you at every moment of the afternoon?'

'Well, I don't know about . . . '

'Because otherwise one could wonder whether you and Ralph argued, and then you followed him here and viciously struck him down, leaving him here to die.'

Ivo blinked, and although his mouth worked, no sound issued.

Reeve Miria sucked at his teeth. 'I find this very interesting. I think I should come with you and speak to the market people. If no one can confirm your story, Ivo, I think you could be in a difficult position.'

Ivo glanced at him sideways, when Peter was looking away, and John saw him make a gesture towards his purse. Reeve Miria's expression didn't alter, but John was sure that he moved his head just a fraction, scarcely enough for anyone to have noticed, but John was half expecting it; there were so many stories about the Reeve's corruption flying about the town. He reflected that he should warn Peter about the Reeve, but then he almost smiled at such a fatuous thought: Peter would already have heard of it.

The Reeve cleared his throat. 'We should get back to town, then. Try to check this man's story.'

'For one, I am glad that the matter is resolved so quickly,' said Eustace Joce. He snorted and yawned. 'I for one have work to be getting on with. I have some sheep with something that looks nasty. I only hope to Christ Jesus that it's not another murrain.'

John shivered at the mere word. In 1315 and 1316, there had been a terrible famine which had affected all, the highest and the lowest in the land, and at the same time there had been a disease among first the sheep, then the cattle all over the country. It lasted years, and all farmers were petrified at the thought that it might recur. Even the abbey's flocks had been decimated.

'I hope your animals are safe,' Peter said earnestly. 'It would be awful to have another instance of disease amongst the animals. I shall suggest a prayer to the Abbot.'

'That is good of you, brother,' Eustace said, and cast a smug look at Ivo. 'Come, Anastasia. We should return.'

'Hmm?' Peter looked up as though surprised. 'I should be most grateful if you could remain a little longer, friend. Or I should say, "friends". There is much to be considered. For example, I noticed how sad you were, maid, on hearing that this man was dead.'

'I do not like to think of a man dying,' Anastasia said with gentle compassion and a quick look at the corpse.

She was a most attractive woman to John's eyes. Her features were pleasingly regular like the Madonna's, her complexion sweetly pale and set off by a clean white wimple which decorously concealed her hair. Only a few strands of a magnificent chestnut hue escaped, gleaming auburn in the sun. She looked delicate, with a broad forehead and eyebrows which arched in crescents over large green eyes. Her mouth was well shaped, if John was any judge, with full and soft-looking lips. As for the rest of her body, he preferred not to permit his eyes to commit the sins of lust or covetousness, but it was impossible not to notice the firm, rounded swelling under her bodice or the swaying of her hips. She was indeed beautiful, and when she turned her eyes upon Peter, he studied her with a smile, as though considering her for the first time.

'The world would be a better place if there was a little more Christian sympathy,' her husband said shortly.

He was a good looking man, John thought. Powerful and well-proportioned, he was a contrast to Peter, with his appalling wound. Apparently Peter thought the same, for he looked away as though ashamed.

'Tell me, maid: did you know this Ralph well?'

'Not particularly, brother.'

'No? Your accent shows you come from this town, though. Were you born here?'

'Yes. But what of it?'

'Surely Ralph lived here all his life as well. And you and he were of an age, weren't you?'

She threw her husband a faintly perplexed smiled, as though wondering where this interrogation was leading.

'What are you talking about, brother?' Eustace grated. 'My wife is here because you asked her here, not for any other reason.'

John privately wondered as much. Anastasia was so pretty a thing, it was impossible to consider that she could have wielded a stone heavy enough to smash Ralph's head. Compared to her mild mannered responses, Peter's questioning sounded harsh and almost cruel.

Peter sighed. 'I was only wondering whether your wife could have known Ralph. She was surely not acquainted with him for the first time today. Even if one sees a dead body by the side of the road, it would not normally lead to tears, would it? Not unless the dead man was personally known to us. That is why I wished to verify that your wife actually knew him.'

Having stated his piece, he looked away again, but this time John could see that his eyes were not unfocussed, gazing into nothingness, but were concentrating with an almost furious anger on Ralph's head. He was a man possessed by an idea, John thought, and such a pure, perfect idea that it would not admit of any other to enter his head.

'If you demand to know, then yes, I knew him,' Anastasia said, with a smile that captivated John. 'We grew up together.'

'What has this to do with the man's murder?' Eustace demanded. His face was red now, as though he was feeling the barb of an insult.

Peter looked to him. 'Why should you feel that it has anything to do with Ralph's death? I have not said that any of my questions are related to Ralph, and yet you seem to feel threatened. Why should that be?'

'I? Threatened? Ballocks to you, my fine brother! I know your sort. You are only a feeble charity-giver, aren't you? Well in my experience, the charity-giver is often the receiver of charity himself! If you didn't have that wound, you wouldn't be here, would you?'

Peter gazed at him directly then, and a blaze of rage, so pure and unfettered that John thought it could have melted lead, leapt from his eyes. Eustace recoiled, a hand rising as though to protect himself, but then, as soon as it flared, Peter's anger dissipated. 'You think I am a weakling, generously protected by the Abbot against the cruelty of the world, Master Joce? Perhaps you are right. I am a sad old man, when all is said and done.'

'My apologies, brother. I didn't think what I was saying,' Eustace Joce said.

Liar! John thought to himself. You said what you thought you needed to distract Peter from your wife, didn't you?

'That's perfectly all right, Master Joce,' Peter said with a sigh. And then he turned back to Anastasia. 'Since you knew him so well, maid, when did you last meet him?'

'Brother, I will not have you interrogating my wife like this!' Eustace exploded immediately. 'This is ridiculous! A man is found up here, dead, and you leap to conclusions, demanding to conduct your own inquest — well, I won't be a part of it, that's all I can say!'

He span on his heel and called to his wife. Anastasia threw him a look of . . . what: gratitude? John wondered . . . and was about to follow him, when Peter called to them.

'Master Joce, please do not go now. There are other matters I would discuss with you.'

'I don't have time for all this.'

'Master, please,' Peter sighed. 'Speedier to answer questions now than to wait and explain in court.'

'What does that mean?' Eustace demanded angrily, spinning to face the old monk.

'The good Abbot has asked me to report to him, and I have a duty to weigh all the facts. If someone refuses to answer my questions, I would have to recommend that the Abbot had him arrested on suspicion at least until the Coroner arrives.'

'You . . . '

'My friend, I have no choice. You must see that,' Peter said placatingly, 'I am a servant to my Lord Abbot.'

Eustace's mouth snapped shut and he took a deep breath. 'You already have your man. Ivo had a dispute with him: surely he was the murderer.'

'I never did a thing to him!' Ivo declared angrily.

'Enough!' the Reeve said, stepping between the two as they squared up to each other. 'Calm down and listen to the monk.'

'Although one man might appear to have a motive, so may another, do you not think?'

'I don't understand what you're getting at,' Eustace said. 'And I don't see why I should waste time listening to this rubbish.'

For the first time Peter's voice hardened. 'Then stop behaving like a cretin, and listen! You may learn something! Now, maid, did . . .'

'No! If you have any questions, you can ask me,' Eustace declared, putting a hand on his wife's forearm.

'Very well. When did you first suspect you were being cuckolded by Ralph?'

Eustace gasped and he shivered, once, convulsively. 'Who told you that?'

'It is common knowledge you will not let your wife out of your sight.'

'That means nothing!'

'No, but your response here, today, does. Would not a man who thought his wife was sleeping with another seek to end their affair? He might kill the man, his wife, or both, but few men would allow the situation to continue.'

'I didn't kill him.'

'But you did suspect that he might have captured a small part of your wife's heart, didn't you? That much is obvious.'

'I . . .' he threw an anxious look at his wife. 'I wondered, that is all.'

She smiled then, but this was not the gentle, soft-featured woman whom John had admired only a few minutes before. Now Anastasia wore a harsh expression, and instead of a gentle Madonna, John thought she looked more like a vicious harlot, a cruel and manipulative Herodias plotting a vengeful death.

'So you accuse my husband of killing him, Brother?'

'It would not be surprising if he did, maid. You sought to make your husband jealous, didn't you?'

'My husband is a poor fool if he thought I desired Ralph. What would I have done with such a pathetic creature? He was dim, an unreliable fool! The only thing he was good for, or good at, was hitting people. He was a brute, no less a brute than that monster of a dog of his: Rumon! Naming a dog after a saint is as sinful as naming a child after a demon! Both are evil, both are heretical.'

'Tell me, maid - St Rumon. What was he made saint for?' Peter asked in his most courteous voice.

Anastasia blinked, shot a glance at her husband, then squared her shoulders defiantly. 'I can't remember.'

'Neither can I,' Peter confessed happily. 'So if we are so heretical as to have forgotten that, perhaps Ralph could be forgiven for naming his dog after the man. At least his dog is loyal,' he said thoughtfully, glancing at the dog. He shook his head a moment, then peered back at the woman. 'Why do you dislike the man so much, maid? Had he upset you?'

'He was nothing to me,' she declared.

'Curious,' Peter said thoughtfully. 'I once spoke to him, and he told me that he had been married. He wedded for love, although the woman died during the famine. Who would she have been? Reeve, do you remember her?'

'Yes. Cristine, her name was, a pretty, fair haired girl, as slim and as fresh and as lovely as a small white rose. All the men loved her.'

'And she died young, I suppose?' Peter asked.

'Too young. So many died too early in those terrible years.'

'Were you jealous of her?' Peter suddenly shot out, staring at Anastasia.

She sneered at him. 'Of her? Marrying that?'

'Show some respect for the man, woman!' Reeve Miria said. 'It's his corpse lying there!'

'Why should I show him anything but contempt? I never liked the man.'

'I thought you had once been sworn to marry him,' Peter said gently.

Eustace stared at him, and for a moment John thought he was going to leap upon the brother. His face mottled with anger, and his hand rested briefly on his sword, but his wife put her hand on his, stilling the blade in the sheath.

'Yes, it's true enough,' she said quietly.

John was shivering with nervous excitement as the little group calmed, but also with a faint fear that Peter was possessed of supernatural powers. It seemed as though Peter was able to guess at people's innermost thoughts and rip from them their darkest secrets.

'Thank you, mistress,' Peter said, this time with a bow to honour her confession.

'I did not kill him,' she said. 'But I hated him from the moment that he betrayed me to Cristine. I suppose I should have been grateful to her. She saved me from marrying him. Still, all I knew was, he had given me his word that he would marry me, and he reneged on it. Cristine and I grew up together, and she had been my best friend, and suddenly, he went with her and made his vows at the church door in front of the parson and the congregation. His words to me were conveniently forgotten.'

Her husband stared at her. 'But I thought you were in love with him again? You spoke much of him when his wife died.'

'Yes, we should consider you, Eustace, shouldn't we?' Peter said. 'Because you knew your wife had loved this man, didn't you?'

'I still don't see that my family's affairs are any of your business,' Eustace returned, but with less anger than before.

'I merely wish to resolve some problems,' Peter said with a calm smile.

Eustace studied him in silence for a long moment, then, 'I knew she had loved him, yes. I grew up in Tavistock with both of them. It would have been difficult not to notice how fond they were of each other.'

'And then Cristine married him, and you saw your opportunity to marry the woman you had adored for years,' Peter said, with a wistful tone to his voice, John thought, as though he had experienced the same chance himself.

'Yes. I never had cause to regret my offer of marriage,' Eustace stated stoutly.

'Until recently, when you began to suspect that Anastasia might be carrying on an affair with Ralph.'

'I wondered, that is all. We have been married seven years now, and I suppose it is natural for a man and his wife to become a little less romantic, but I thought there was a problem.'

Anastasia turned her astonished face to him. 'You seriously thought I would consider an affair with a rough, dirty fellow like Ralph?'

'I didn't know what to think,' Eustace muttered. 'All I was convinced of was that you were less affectionate to me.'

'Oh, husband! I need affection too. I thought if you were jealous of another man, you might show me more.'

'Why? Are you so insecure?'

'I am pregnant!'

Eustace's mouth gaped wide. 'Are you sure?' he asked.

A little of the steeliness returned to her face, but only for a moment. Then she smiled. 'Yes, husband, I am.'

'That's wonderful news,' Peter said warmly. 'Congratulations! Um. But where were you last afternoon, master Eustace?'

'I? I was at the market, at my stall. I would think that almost everyone in the town could confirm that. Including the Reeve here, because you came to buy some eggs and a lamb with your lady, didn't you, Robert?'

Peter looked at the Reeve, and there was a glitter in his eyes which reminded John of the times when the old monk had caught one of the novices with his hand in the biscuit jar. 'Is that so, Reeve?'

Reeve Miria shrugged. 'Yes. I was there most of the afternoon, apart from a short space when I had to go home.'

'On business?' Peter enquired.

'Yes.'

'Such as, for example, asking for a loan to be repaid?'

'A man of business has so many affairs it's sometimes hard to remember them all,' Miria said loftily.

'Perhaps you should try to exercise your mind, then, Reeve,' Peter said. 'Could it have been a meeting to talk about calling in a debt, do you think? Perhaps - correct me on this - but could it have been a loan to Ralph, for example?'

John felt his brows leap upwards in surprise as though they were on springs. Turning to face the Reeve, he saw that the man had blenched, and he fiddled with the thong that bound his swordbelt.

'He come by at one point.'

'Early in the afternoon, wasn't it?'

'I think it might have been.'

'So you could have had plenty of time to follow him here, strike him down, and return to town to fulfil your duties as Reeve.'

'To ride all the way here and back? And I didn't even know he'd be coming up here. How could I?'

'Maybe he mentioned he was coming here. It was part of his bailiwick, and he was always happy to talk about his work.'

'I did nothing wrong,' the Reeve said.

'Nothing? Even though you wanted to make profit from lending money? You were committing usury, Reeve. That is wrong. Jesus taught that it's sinful to make money from money. If you have enough, any spare is God's gift. Using that to make profit is an abuse of his plenty, and that is a most serious crime. You demanded his loan to be returned, even though you knew he couldn't afford it.'

'I did what any man of business would have done.'

'Perhaps in future you'll consider doing what a man of Christian spirit would do,' Peter snapped. His bushy eyebrows had dropped and now they all but concealed his eyes. Only an occasional glitter shone from them.

Then he took a deep breath. 'Look at us all. Here we stand: one man who had a perpetual battle with him because of some rabbits; another who feared that Ralph wanted to steal his wife; the wife who hated him and wanted revenge for not marrying her, but who now was more concerned about her pregnancy than her husband; the Reeve who wanted profit, and damn any man who wouldn't repay his debts even though the Reeve was not himself in need. This is a sad, terrible matter. I must pray and contemplate. John, come with me.'

He turned abruptly and crossed the clapper bridge, swiftly putting yards between them and the silent and ashamed group. Without turning, he said, 'Have any of them followed us?'

'No.'

'Good.'

Peter suddenly grabbed John's upper arm and stared at him keenly. 'Boy, whatever you do now, do not lie to me! I wanted all those to be here because I thought one of them had killed Ralph. I drank with him yesterday at an alehouse after he had met the Reeve, and I knew that each of them hated him. He told me so. After I left him, he came straight to the moors to check on his bailiwick. Some of those back there could have come here and killed him, but it's not likely. However the chance of a lad seeing him, now that is quite possible.'

His eyes were intense chips of diamond. They cut into John as he spoke.

'Boy, did you meet Ralph yesterday? Don't lie to me, because if you do, I shall punish you myself, and you'll regret it if I do. You were up here, weren't you? Yesterday, like today, you rode up here to exercise the horse, but also to see if you could have some sport. It's illegal to be up here, we all know that, but if a Forester like Ralph saw you, he'd threaten you with immediate exposure to the Abbot. Is that what happened? And then you hit him?'

John gaped, and such was the strength of his emotion, he felt the tears begin to fall. He couldn't speak; his tongue was frozen and he was too shocked to deny Peter's words.

'I see, boy. Well, no need to say more. I shan't propose to hold these others any longer. I understand. Come!'

He turned and walked back to the bridge, John following with his mind whirling and eyes streaming.

It was this that prevented him from seeing the disaster. As Peter climbed onto the clapper bridge, John sniffed and rubbed his eyes. Afterwards Peter wondered whether there was a similar command that the Forester had used for his mastiff, a signal that could be used silently at night to show Rumon what he wanted; whatever the reason, Rumon caught sight of John's arms up at his face and instantly gave a joyful bark. He sprang up and leapt forward as Peter reached the middle of the bridge, and bounded on, over the bridge, and to John.

'No!'

John heard the cry, but he had no eyes for anyone or anything other than the monster suddenly thundering towards him. He saw huge, pendulous jowls flying in the wind, drool trailing; he saw a slobbering tongue; ripples of sagging flesh moving with each step like waves on the sea; and then the creature was on him, knocking his legs away, and panting happily over him, tongue swabbing his throat and cheeks like pumice.

No one came to help him, and it was some time before he could push, curse and kick the dog from him and stand again. Realising at last that this was no a reincarnation of his master, the dog sat again, cowed, and only then could John turn his attention back to the crowd.

He saw Anastasia, he saw the Reeve and Ivo, he saw Eustace, but where he expected to see Peter, there was nothing. Only two legs waving in the air near the bridge.

'Will one of you moronic, demented, poxed sons of a Carlisle whore come and help me up?' came Peter's voice, roaring with an entirely unfeigned fury.

'So that was that,' Peter said later as he and John sat at their fire. The rest had departed, all strangely muted after their confessions of the afternoon.

'Why did you want all those people up here?' John asked.

'They could any one of them have killed him. It was possible. Yet I wanted to show each that their motives were not good. Ivo wanted to kill the dog - is that justification for murder? He never tried to get on with Ralph. At least now, I hope, he will consider his behaviour and moderate it in future. Eustace I know has been jealous of his wife for years and it is about time he grew out of it. She is not so faithless as to throw herself at another man; although she could well seek revenge for a slight. And what worse slight could a woman receive than that the man she sought to marry should take her best friend instead?'

'What of the Reeve?'

Peter chuckled. 'He's no murderer! But I detest this modern practice of seeking reward for that which God has granted. I tweaked the tail of his pride. Maybe in future he'll charge lower interest.'

'And me?'

Peter smiled grimly, perhaps with a faint indication of remorse. 'There are times when even the best cleric makes mistakes. I thought that you were up here, and I saw that if you had met the Forester you could have been in great trouble, so it was possible that you could have grabbed a rock and stunned him. If he fell in the water, he would drown, but I was prepared to give you the benefit of the doubt and assume you hadn't intended to kill him.'

'Whereas in fact . . .'

'Whereas in fact it was his faithful dog.' Peter reached over and rubbed the mastiff's head. 'I wondered about that as soon as we arrived here. If a man had knocked Ralph down, I would have expected a dog like this to defend him. At the least I would have expected to find some material from a man's coat nearby, bitten from him by the brute - but there was nothing! That should have proved it, I suppose, but you never can be sure, and some of the largest beasts I have seen have also been the most mild.'

'So how did Ralph die?'

'You saw what happened to me. Suppose Rumon saw a rabbit when Ralph was halfway over the bridge? He is a clumsy, lumbering monster, so, as he passed over the bridge, he clipped Ralph's legs just as he did mine, and Ralph toppled headfirst into the stream. He struck his head and was dazed, so when his head went under the water, he couldn't save himself. That was that.'

'Dying here all alone.'

'Aye, with his killer: the only creature in the world who loved him without reservation.'

DANCE OF DEATH

It was a year of horror, the year of the Great Death: 1348, a year in which men died choking in the streets, and none would go to ease their suffering or soothe their anguish. Even priests dared not speak to them or give them extreme unction. The *pestis atra*, or *atra mors*, the physicians called it.

But merely calling it 'dreadful' could not convey its full horror. People would fall prey to a fever, coughing and spitting blood, and would be dead in a day or two. Others would grow strange lumps—buboes—in armpits or groins, and these would be dead within a week. For a time, the whole city of Exeter reeked of the stench of death and decay.

Yet it was the other death that would stay in David's mind. While others concentrated on their personal woes, David could think only of him: the boy who had appeared with the pilgrims, and who had died so swiftly. The boy who had heralded the deaths throughout the city.

Ten years ago now, that had been. But those who had lived through the plague would always remember.

For David, it had began on one cool, dry evening in early September, in the twenty-first year of the reign of King Edward III.

David rose from his labours, rubbing at his leg. The act of bending to weed his strip in the vill's fields had made all his muscles ache, taut as bowstrings, and he felt older than his fifty-first year.

"Are you well, Father?"

The young novice Luke, tawny-haired like a lion, with the thin features and slim build of a peasant, leaned on his hoe and peered at him anxiously.

"Of course, I am well!" David snapped, and then seeing the hurt on Luke's face, he felt foolish. It was easy to upset Luke. It was as easy as kicking a puppy. "It is just this work, Luke. It occasionally hurts. It reminds me of my old injury."

Two and twenty years before, it had been, when he had received the wound that had marked him for life. He had been a young fellow then, and strong for a priest. His family were nobles, his father a knight, and he had had the great fortune to be placed in the *familia* of the great Bishop Walter of Exeter.

But not all had loved Bishop Walter. While on a visit to London, David was present when the bishop was torn from his horse. Without even giving him a chance to pray for his soul, the mob had beheaded him and left his body in the street. David, his blood boiling, had done all he might to save his bishop, but against so many, there was little he could achieve. His efforts had been rewarded with a beating, and a blow from an iron-shod staff had shattered his leg. It was fortunate that he had survived at all, although with a limp.

It was truly a terrible age. He remembered when he was a boy, studying under Bishop Walter's pupil-master at Exeter and heard a priest whispering that the end of the world must soon come. Rumours of the Pope murdering his predecessor were rife, and the destruction of the Knights Templar had shaken Christendom no less than the loss of the Holy Land.

Even now, David could remember that priest's soft words: "If one would seek to learn what the Lord God thinks of His Christians, one need only look to Jerusalem. He took it from us and gave it to heathens!"

Aye, he thought. Christians slew his bishop, the Pope himself was guilty of murder, and all over the world, Christians blasphemed, murdered, fornicated or worse. It was no surprise that God sought to punish the world with a great pestilence.

Luke was still looking at him. David gave him a conciliatory duck of his head and returned to his work, hoeing between the kale.

It was not long after that the party of refugees appeared at St. Petrock's Gate.

They were sixteen in all: a scruffy group of men, women, and children, clad in greys and russets, one or two with a flash of brighter colour. But it was not the colour that attracted David's eye; it was their drawn, fretful expressions. They had the look of people who had seen their own death.

"Who are they, Father?" Luke asked.

"People who have seen the pestilence."

The year before, the first rumours had come of the spread of a dreadful disease all over the East, and to their shame, many had immediately crowed to hear that their enemies had suffered this catastrophe. Some even suggested that God was seeking to eradicate all heretics, and that removing Christians from Jerusalem was merely for their own protection before He offered them the whole of the Holy Land, free of the infestation of Moors and Mongols.

But that confidence wilted as tales arrived of ships reaching ports nearer and nearer to England. Ships full of corpses, or with the dying sprawled in their own filth, their flesh suppurating. And then they heard that whole cities had fallen prey to the plague. Thousand, tens of thousands, were dead in cities from Italy to the French coast.

Then, at last, it reached England.

Some thought it had arrived in Bristol, while others said it was somewhere in Dorset. David had heard stories of a ship in Dartmouth bringing the first corpses and the port reeve having the ship towed out to sea. But wherever it had first appeared, it had taken hold in no time.

"Will it come here, Father?" Luke asked.

"It is in God's hands, Luke. It's not for us to worry. We must keep to our Cheryl and pray that He will protect our institution. We can do no more."

"I am scared, Father."

"So are many, but there is little need. God will protect us until He decides to take us to His peace."

Luke seemed content with that. He nodded and bent once more to his task, but David stood staring at the knot of travellers standing confused near the gate. He wondered what they had seen. Men, women, and children died every day, but this was different. There was no protection from it. All who came close fell before its virulence. Physicians going to treat patients would die before their patients. Mothers treating their children, fathers seeking help for a devastated hamlet—all were dying.

And there was nothing anyone could do.

"Father, God's grace be on you," the first man said as David approached the group. He was short, with a slight hunch to his back like a man used to carrying a heavy load, but his hands were clean. This was no peasant. "Could I beg a sup of water?"

"Friends, you may take all you can drink," David said. He rolled his shoulders to ease them a little and led the way to the conduit. Water was brought to the cathedral close by means of underground passages and pipes, arriving here at the circular pool where servants would collect it. David scooped a little and drank from his hand. It was warm, and he was glad his duties in his little garden were done for the day.

He watched while the man took a goatskin and held the spout to the water.

"Where are you from?" David asked.

"I"ve come from Rookford." He was named Piers, he said, and had been reeve of the manor. Now there was no manor to serve. He shook the skin and plugged it. Like a man fearful of admitting his own guilt, he averted his eyes, staring anywhere but at the vicar. David had seen this before: survivors who often felt that living when others died was a source of shame.

A woman said, "We are on pilgrimage: We will persuade God to take pity on us!"

"The plague?" David asked more quietly. The other pilgrims possessed the same weary emptiness that he had once seen in the faces of refugees during the civil wars of his youth.

The man nodded and looked away. "We heard of the pestilence approaching— who hasn't?—but we hoped against hope that it would pass us by. In Crediton, it passed through like fire on dry thatch. Not a family was safe against it. I lost all. My wife, my two sons ..."

"It has scourged all Devon," David said. "I pray that God will relent and forgive us."

"He will not," Piers said. His eyes were filled with dread. "He will destroy all of us. We do not deserve His forgiveness. All we do demonstrates our guilt."

David frowned a moment. "What do you mean?"

"We are all sinners," the man said. "All of us. Why should God show us mercy?"

"Aye, that we are," David said, but he watched with a faint frown as the man shouldered his skin once more and rejoined his companions.

Later, David and Luke were given ale to share among the pilgrims. They had been housed in a large room where they could shed their boots, and now many sat and rubbed blistered feet and ankles.

David studied them carefully as he walked amongst them. There were plenty of stories of the symptoms afflicting those who would die: the coughing, the fevers, the swellings that invariably heralded death. To his relief, none here showed any sign of such afflictions. There were no foul buboes, only good, healthful blisters and bloody sores.

"We all decided to leave when it was clear what was happening. We thought to save ourselves," Reeve Piers said. There was a haunted look still in his eyes as he spoke. He should have remained at the manor until his lord could return, but he had not. He had fled like all the others, leaving the manor prey to draw-latches and thieves. It would not go well with him when his master returned to find the place ravaged or levelled.

But Piers plainly guessed it was unlikely his master would return. "When so many had already died, we thought it best to fly. But where can we go? There is nowhere safe."

"There is always hope, my friend," David said.

"You have not lost all," Piers said flatly.

A dark-haired woman looked up. She had a heart-shaped face and large, fearful eyes raw with weeping. Speaking quietly, she said, "I have lost my husband, my son, and two brothers. You think I should have hope? No one should have to see such sights. I saw my neighbour try to give her baby pap, and next day, I heard the babe bawling, but when I looked, her mother was dead. The husband had already died. I wanted to go to the child, but what could I do? I have been dry for these last five years. I couldn't wet-nurse."

David heard the defensiveness in her voice. She had not dared go to the baby. It must have died slowly of hunger.

Another man spoke. He was huddled like an old peasant near a fire, elbows on knees, his chin resting on his fists. His gaze was fixed on some far-distant horizon. "All my children. Wife, friends, all. We were living at Henstill, close by Rookford. All dead now. None left. What hope do *I* have?"

David struggled with something to soothe them, but could think of nothing in the face of their despair. He nodded to Luke, who went to fetch more ale. At least, they could help these poor travellers forget.

It was two days later that news came of the first of the deaths near the city at Heavitree.

David was surprised to be called to the chapter house with vicars and canons alike. Usually the chapter would meet to discuss duties, and after that, the meeting would continue with only the dean and senior clergy. Today, all were called to be present.

"What is happening, Father?" Luke asked.

David wanted to say, "What do you think?" but he had to clench his jaw. Was the boy so dense that he had not heard the news? Surely even the dullest village fool would guess.

The chapter house was surging with tension. As more men entered, the anticipation rose, climbing and climbing, until David felt sure that some of the older men must die from the strain.

At last, Dean John walked in. He had the look of a man who had sat up till late at night with a barrel of good wine. His eyes had great bruises beneath them, and his manner, abrupt at the best of times, was disjointed as he spoke.

"You will ... we have all, I suppose, heard of the pestilence that assails our kingdom. It is, it has ..." The dean broke off, staring about him at all the chapter with eyes full of confusion. He was too old to cope with this crisis, David realized. He wished the precentor or the treasurer would save Dean John the trouble of explaining the case.

The old dean tottered, but continued after a moment or two. "My brothers, it ... that is, we, now have to reconcile ourselves to the disaster falling about our ears. We must ... we have choices. Decisions. My God! That I should live to see such times!"

The precentor at last rose, took the dean's arm, and led him to a bench on which he could rest. Standing beside him, the precentor looked almost a boy, although he was in his late twenties.

"We must immediately arrange for public prayers. I will call for processions on every Wednesday, and until this pestilence ends, we must hold masses of the utmost gravity to demonstrate our piety. Everything must be done to demonstrate to God how deeply we wish to ..."

Saul, an ancient priest, jerked to his feet suddenly, his thin, pale face tragic. While his filmy eyes stared about him wildly at all the canons and priests, he tore at his lank white hair. "We know what's led to this!" he shouted, his reedy voice full of passion. "The Pope and all his cardinals have brought us to this because of their wickedness and greed! Their betrayal of the Knights Templar, their arrogance, their pride, their avarice—and their murder! They murdered Pope Celestine V, of blessed memory, because he was a saintly man! They have taken God's perfect world and His people and made use of them, ignoring His instructions, ignoring His …"

His voice broke, and he fell to his knees on the hard stone flags as he finished his peroration, while uproar broke out. Canons and vicars argued loudly about the Pope and his predecessors, while the precentor and two custors tried to call them to order. The frustration and anxiety of past weeks overwhelmed even them, and as two servants hurried to Saul's side, taking him by the arms and pulling him towards the door, David feared that his companions might yet come to blows. But then at the door, Saul turned and shouted. The Chapter was startled into silence as he spoke again.

"It is the end of the world, Brothers! Famine, war, and plague! We have seen the famine, we have experienced war, and now we must perish in the last!"

A short while before the locking of the gates to the cathedral's close, David saw the shambling boy enter.

He was only eleven or twelve years old, and had the emaciated appearance of a peasant's son. David saw him while he stood in the Broad Gate, staring about him with the wide-eyed look of a boy who had never seen such a building before and was struck dumb with awe.

The lad had probably never seen a city before, David thought to himself.

He limped across to the boy. "My son, do you seek someone?"

The boy looked up at him with empty eyes that seared David's soul. Then he registered the bloody scab on the boy's temple. He felt the breath catch in his throat at the sight. "My son, come with me. You need food and water. I can offer you both."

Nodding dumbly, the child trailed after him as David took him first to the clerk of the bread chest, persuading him to give up one small loaf, and thence to a bench near the conduit. The boy sat and tore at the loaf, stuffing it into his mouth in chunks that could have choked him, had not David persuaded him to slow and drink some water to wash it down.

"What's your name?" he asked when the boy finished eating. David saw Luke and sent him scurrying off to fetch clean cloth and some oil of lavender.

"Thomas."

"Where are you from?"

The boy looked up at David. "Rookford." His eyes rose to the cathedral before them. "Did God build that?"

"He did, in a way," David smiled. "You shall see inside it." Just then Luke returned, and David moistened a cloth in water, sprinkling a little lavender on it to wipe away the filth from the boy's brow. It was as he worked that he said. "Rookford? Is that the vill near Crediton?"

"Yes. But it is empty now. All have died or fled."

David beamed as he finished cleaning the wound. It was heavily bruised, but Thomas would heal. The young always did. "This is wonderful! Some people from there arrived only yesterday! The reeve and some other —"

"Reeve Piers is here?" the boy said sharply. "Where?"

His excitement was natural, and David thought nothing of it. He at once stood and beckoned, leading the way to the cathedral's north door. Inside, the boy stood still again, struck dumb with awe at the sight of the soaring ceiling, the vast empty expanse of the nave. Some men stood negotiating business transactions, while others knelt on the hard stone paving, heads bent, their hands clasped in penitence and pleading. All around the walls, others murmured their *Pater Nosters* while fondling their beads.

David was struck with the feeling that this space could give comfort to even the most tragic soul. Here the troubles of the world were dissipated, taken away by God's grace, and leaving the poor people eased.

In recent weeks, the church had been filled like this at all times of the day. As news of the pestilence approached ever nearer, people came here seeking the peace that only God could bring. Many brought their fears and terrors and found that they could leave them behind, outside the cathedral doors. In the chapels, men and women would listen to the masses and feel the comfort of God's words.

In the Chapel of St. Edmund, David saw the reeve kneeling, head bowed, his body wracked with silent sobs, the other pilgrims of his party nearby. At his side was the woman. It was a sight to tear at the heart.

"Come, child. The reeve from your vill is here," he said softly.

There was a sudden change in the boy's eyes as he drew his gaze away from the monumental stonework and brought his attention back to earth. David was struck by his appearance. "Is there something the matter?"

"Where is he? Take me to him!"

David felt a prickle of uneasiness, but he pointed and began to march the boy to St. Edmund's altar. Before he had covered three paces, the boy stopped. "Father!" he shouted on seeing the reeve and bolted to him.

It was hard to believe that a lad so scrawny could cover the ground so quickly. He sped over it with such haste that he knocked one elderly woman from her feet in his headlong rush. David was struck with the feeling that he ought to run to stop the boy. But even as he told himself that this was just the joy of a lad who saw friends at last after a journey through the horrors of a countryside filled with the dead and dying, he forced down a sick sensation in his stomach: a growing conviction that something was wrong.

Then he heard the scream from the reeve and saw the knife flash once, twice, in the boy's hand. He picked up his tunic and hurried to the altar as fast as his ruined leg would allow him.

He was glad to see Luke reach the boy and grasp his arm before he could strike a third time, but even as he did so, the woman at Reeve Pier's side gave a moan and collapsed, her hand at her breast as she fell to the floor, her blood spreading over the flags.

The dean peered at the reeve on his narrow bed in the infirmary. "You are sure of this?"

"How can I not? I must confess my crimes, and there can be no better place."

The reeve had been roughly stitched where the boy's blade had raked along his breast, baring two ribs. Now the infirmarer had bandaged the wound, and the dean, with David, Luke, and a custor, stood at the bedside.

"I will listen."

Luke stood near the boy in case he tried anything else. The dean glanced at David and the others as though gauging their strength. Turning back to the man, he nodded. "Continue."

"I am the reeve to Sir John de Sully at Rookford. He has been away these last months, first with the King in France, and more recently at London. When the plague appeared, we had no help. We had no idea where to turn. People fell about us. Helen, the wife of a local farmer, saw her family die about her, and those of her neighbours. She told you about the woman's babe?" he said, appealing to David.

"She did."

"It was clear that the whole vill was dying. There was nothing left, and I thought it would be best if at least some of us survived. So I persuaded some to join me and come away."

"To save them?" the dean asked, nodding.

Piers looked up at him, but it was David who spoke, "No, Dean. Not to save them. To satisfy his own urges. Isn't that true?"

"Yes," Piers said. His eyes were filled with tears. "You condemn me, but you don't know what it was like! You can't understand! The vill was condemned already. All of us had lost our friends and families. We were desperate."

David stared at him. There was more to this than the reeve admitted, he was sure. "Tell us all, as you want salvation."

The reeve turned a face of such despair to him that David almost felt remorse for forcing him to admit what he had done. It was only the reflection that the confession would save the fellow's soul that hardened his heart.

"After the harvest, we always had a celebration in our vill," the reeve said. "We never got out of hand, but this year, with the news of the pestilence sweeping across the land, I suppose we all felt more uninhibited. While the ale and cider flowed, we all danced and enjoyed ourselves. But my wife and I had argued, and at the end, I found myself in a chamber with Helen. She was full of ale, too, and we did what a man and woman will."

"You took advantage of her?" the dean said uncompromisingly. His face was pale as he listened. "You forced her to commit adultery?"

"There was no force needed on either hand. We had both known each other for years. I watched her from a distance with admiration. It never occurred to me that she … Anyway, when my wife was dead, I thought we should leave. My sons were dead, I thought –"

"You decided to leave your vill and all the people in it," the dean stated.

"I brought all the people I thought were alive."

"But your son was not dead."

"I thought he was. Helen told me he was. She wanted to get away, she said, to start a new family with me. It was all her fault! I would never have left my boy!"

"And you didn't think to check on him yourself?"

"You cannot understand! Everyone was dying! We packed what we could and left."

David joined Thomas later out by the conduit and gathered together the shards of the story, Luke at his side.

"You are the reeve's son?" David said quietly.

"His second, yes. My elder brother was his favourite, but Peter died when the plague first came to afflict us, two weeks ago. Since then, my father has shown me no kindness. He would have preferred me to die, rather than Peter. I wish *I* had died instead!"

"What happened?"

"The vill was hit hard. The grown men all died, and so did many women. Mother was one of the few who survived. But so did Helen. Father had adored her for many years and wanted her, but he dared not try anything while her husband was alive. And then when she was widowed and her children died, my father took her."

"But your mother, too, was dead."

"Is that what he said?" Thomas gaped. "It's a lie! He *murdered* her!"

"You know this?"

"Mother sent me to find him, and I was told he was in Helen's house. I found him there, with *her*. He was rutting on her like a ram on a ewe. I just stood staring and he saw me. He was like a man gone mad! Foaming at the mouth, berserk. He leaped from her and rushed at me. It was all I could do to jump through the door, but he caught me and hit me with a club. He gave me this," Thomas said, touching the scab at his brow gingerly. "And then he killed my mother. He slew her as a butcher would slay a hog: He cut her throat."

Luke gave a short gasp, but David shushed him. "You are sure of this?"

"I found her. But all the rest were flown. They went with him. He told them that the vill was cursed, that all would die if they remained there. The plague would find them out and they must perish. And he was their reeve, so they trusted him. He led them all away, and they believed in him. They didn't know he was a murderer who killed to satisfy his own lusts!"

"He will pay for his crimes," David said. "He has confessed, and the city will hold him for trial."

"I just want him to suffer for what he did to my mother," Thomas said. He turned away from them. David wanted to put a hand out to him, but something stopped him.

It was then that Thomas gave his first cough. It sounded like a man clearing his throat those first few times, but within the hour, the cough had grown to a harsh hacking that rasped all the way up from his lungs.

The boy Thomas was in the infirmary before noon, and his frail body was shattered by each fresh bout of coughing. By evening of the second day, he was dead.

That was only the beginning. Soon the cathedral was shaken by the tolling of the bells at each fresh influx of corpses. Then the canons and vicars of the cathedral began to die. In a matter of weeks, there were so few that Bishop Grandisson had to petition the Pope for permission to ordain the illegitimate and even men who were underage. The permission was granted; all the Church's institutions were in the same straits.

But the supreme irony for David was that although the boy died, his miserable father was spared. Indeed, when the justices arrived the following year to dispense judgement, not only did they find Piers was still living, they decided that he was innocent. No one had taken an account of the boy's evidence. Only David could speak for Thomas: The dean was dead, as was Luke. Both had died from the pestilence, while the custor had died when he was thrown from his horse. But there was so much death in those days that recording a man's guilt that he might be executed was low on any man's list of priorities.

Could David blame the reeve for his behaviour? A man in a position of respect and authority should be more reliable, it is true, but in those days of despair, when all felt sure that God had deserted them, it was no surprise that a man could be brought so low that he could commit such acts. As for David, he was sure that other crimes had occurred, hidden by the appalling toll of death. So many lost so much that the balance of their minds was disordered. The reeve spent all the rest of his days a broken man, remembering always the sons he had lost, the wife he had murdered, the lover slain by the son he had thought already dead.

What was strange was that David, even after so many years, could not bring Piers's features to mind. Piers was a name, a passing shadow of a memory. A player in the dance of life—and death.

But the son he had tried to kill—that boy's face would stay with David all his life: a boy betrayed by a lustful father, a boy killed unjustly by a hideous pestilence.

Made in the USA
Lexington, KY
21 May 2016